Possum Summer

Jen K. Blom

Holiday House / New York

Acknowledgments

Thanks to my wonderful, brilliant agent Marlene Stringer, whose tenacity is worth its weight in gold. Eternal gratitude also to my sharp-eyed, compassionate editor Julie Amper, who understood my P inside and out, and her colleagues Mary Cash and Sylvie Frank for their roles in *Possum Summer*'s path to publication. *Muchas gracias* goes to Kerri, my diminutive twin, for her stalwart support, as well as my childhood possum (Squiggy) and raccoon (Ikey) for the seeds of this story. Not to forget my own dear Gran. She'd be tickled to know she lives on in these pages.

Text copyright © 2011 by Jen K. Blom
Illustrations copyright © 2011 by Omar Rayyan
All Rights Reserved
HOLIDAY HOUSE is registered in the U.S. Patent and Trademark Office.
Printed and Bound in May 2011 at Maple Vail, York, PA, USA.
www.holidayhouse.com
First Edition
1 3 5 7 9 10 8 6 4 2
Library-of-Congress Cataloging-in-Publication Data
Blom, Jen K.
Possum summer / by Jen K. Blom. — 1st ed.
p. cm.
Summary: While her father is away at war, eleven-year-old Princess ignores his warning that pet ownership leads to pain when she raises an orphaned possum on their Oklahoma ranch, then tries to send it back to the wild.
ISBN 978-0-8234-2331-6 (hardcover)
[1. Opossums—Fiction.   2. Wildlife rescue—Fiction.   3. Orphaned animals—Fiction.   4. Ranch life—Oklahoma—Fiction.   5. Dogs—Fiction.   6. Fathers and daughters—Fiction.   7. Oklahoma—Fiction.]   I. Title.
PZ7.B6198Pos 2011
[Fic]—dc22
2010023476

For Sören, with my love

Chapter 1

I didn't stop to wonder how I was going to save it—or what would happen if I did.

"Drop! *Drop!*" I screeched to Blackie as he stood, worrying his prize by the creek. When he dropped it, startled, and it started floating down the river, I didn't even think once about it. Blasting past him, I shot into the water, cutting myself on shale rocks, slipping on the sandy bottom. I knew this part of the creek good: it didn't come up past my thigh, and the catfish didn't like it 'cause it was too open, so nothing would try to get the possum from below.

I sloshed after it, droplets like diamonds sparkling in every direction. The animal wasn't moving as it bobbed in the water, but there wasn't any time to waste. Idiot dog. I should've left him at home. I wasn't supposed to have him out, anyways.

When I reached it I pulled up short, the strong current swirling around my skinny, berry-stained feet. The possum was floating along, mouth gaping. Drat.

I grabbed a stick and angled the body out of the water, trying to ignore the blood streaming from its belly. Cussing under my breath, I flipped the possum sloppily the last little way out of the water. It landed with a wet thud. I was too late.

I knew dead, and this was it. No faking.

The possum was a rich gray-silver, tipping to black on the

long outside hairs. The wise old face was white as snow, the little fingers softly pink. I felt like crying. This wasn't the first time Blackie had done something like this, but seeing as it was my fault this time, it really got to me. I glared at him as he came wriggling up, his rear end moving all over creation.

"You darn dog, you!" I yelled, and pointed down at the ground to the possum dead at my feet. "That's it! No more comin' out here if you won't listen to me!"

He crawled the last little way to me on his belly, stump tail going a mile a minute. His cheerful eyes met mine. Surely I wasn't mad at him, was I? I almost weakened, but the blood on his mouth just made me so angry.

"Do you see what you did?" I pointed at the possum again. He stood up, glanced at me, and stretched forward to take the possum in his mouth.

I about blew my top. "No!" The possum was dead, but I didn't want him to eat it. "Leave it!" Blackie pulled back from the carcass, looking at me mournfully. He whimpered.

"No! Go on, you're a bad dog!" With a big huffing sigh, he wandered over to the creek and flopped down under a big cottonwood tree. He was panting, his ears pricked up at attention, his intelligent eyes alert. He was a fine-looking dog, a blue heeler, almost black, with one whacky white eye. He was my dad's dog. I could just imagine how angry he'd be if he knew Blackie was with me.

"Come on, P, pull yourself together," I muttered, and grabbed a thick stick to dig into the sand by the creek. As soon as I buried the poor dead thing, we could head home for lunch. My stomach was thinking my throat'd been cut.

As I turned the soft ground, I heard something, a wet sort of rustle. I stood up and looked around suspiciously.

I was miles from home—miles from anything, in fact. What the good old Oklahoma river bottoms teach you is a nice healthy respect for your fellow living creatures. I couldn't count the times I'd been spooked by a snake or skunk or coon, chased by a rogue bull, or treed by a wild pig. You had to keep your wits around you down here, especially with the rabies epidemic traveling through. I turned around slowly, staring the shadows out from under the trees. Nothing. Then I heard the rustling sound again, coming from right at my feet.

I looked down at the possum and dropped the stick. The belly was moving. But it was dead!

"Oh, darn it," I whispered, dropping to my knees. I used a tiny stick to pull a flap of skin away from the animal's gashed-open belly. The possum was dead, but from its pouch, a little baby possum peeked up at me, eyes squinted to slits in the harsh sunlight.

Chapter 2

I reached down real slow, but the little thing just sat there at the tip of the ripped pouch, looking up at me. As I bent down closer I could see the mother's stomach had been slashed open, and I felt a surge of fury at that dumb dog. He'd been after the *babies*.

I looked up and glared at him a minute. He looked at me and moseyed on over, eyes sharpening right up when he saw that baby. Like it was lunch.

"Leave it," I said, using one of Dad's cattle-working words on him. He seemed to respond to work-training words, not the ones I tried to teach him, like *sit* and *shake hands*.

He glanced at me and didn't move, so I bent closer to the baby and reached out a trembling finger to touch its head. The fur was damp, and it pulled wetly to the side as I petted it slowly. Who knew how early a possum kit had teeth? Would it bite? Was it a girl or a boy? I didn't want to look at its private parts. Its face looked to me like he was a boy, so I just decided that's what he was.

He reached his little nose up to meet my finger and sniffed it. Then he licked it. I wanted to wipe my hand on my shorts. He trundled out a little into the sunlight, nose raised as he went, and turned around to look at his mother. He stretched his nose over to her stiff foot and nudged it gently. I think I might have made a sound in my throat. Something whimpered.

He was way too small. He'd never make it out here, especially if he was still nursing. The whole baby wasn't much bigger than a soda pop can, including his long pink tail.

He was a soft gray color, not dark like his mother, but with faint brushes of frosted white tips on his hairs. Shoe-button black eyes surrounded by bright white, the white color of birthday cake icing. It made his face seem cuter than any stuffed animal I'd ever had. I wanted to help him so bad. To save him.

But I'd get skinned alive if I came home with him. Even though my dad wasn't there, wasn't even in the same country, my mama would forbid me to keep him because that's what Dad would have wanted.

Pets are nothing but luxury on a farm, P, he'd say. *Every animal out here needs to earn its keep, kid. Nobody gets a free ride on a cattle ranch. And besides, pets only cause you pain anyways. Trust me.*

He thought it was bad enough I tried to be friends with Blackie, even though the dog mostly just ignored me. Dad believed it would make Blackie soft, turn him off his only purpose—herding the cattle.

I looked down at the possum as he nosed at the sand. His little legs were thinner than my pinkie.

I'd have no help from my mom. And my sister? I huffed, laughing a little as I squatted next to the little possum. She'd turn me in herself, especially if it got her a ride into town, where she always wanted to be. She'd probably be allergic to the possum anyways. So nope, no help there, either.

The urge to take him home laid down on me like one of my gran's Sunday dinners. I just couldn't leave him here, but that didn't help the butterflies inside.

I slapped my palms on my skinned knees, trying to work up the guts to do it. I knew if I picked him up he'd be mine, forever. I took some deep breaths and clenched my fists. Dad wasn't here, Mama was off working all the time, and unless she was going to town, my sister never set foot outside the house because of her allergies to everything.

It was surely worth a shot.

I let out the air I was holding inside with a big rush. He jumped a little and looked at me, his big black eyes glistening, and my heart just melted. I was going to save him. It was my fault that crazy dog had killed his whole family, and doggone it, I was going to keep this little possum, this baby, from dying.

I reached down and picked him up, loving the feel of his little feet pressing into my hand. He settled in, curling up as I covered him with my other hand. His cold nose touched my palm. He was mine!

What little I knew about possums could have curled right up alongside him. I knew they were mostly around in the nighttime; they were foragers; and they played dead a lot. I'd run into them often on my adventures out here. But that was about it.

As I stood up, my toes nudged the possum mama. I couldn't leave her there to rot, or even worse, get chomped on by some animal looking for an easy lunch. I glanced at Blackie.

He now stood a couple feet away, ears pricked, staring at the dead possum. He was drooling, and I knew he'd sneak back and chow down on her if I left her above ground. But where could I put the baby while I buried her?

I stuck the hand holding him gingerly into the pocket of my dirty red shorts. I wiggled it a little, working my hand down deep, and dropped the baby possum in. I jiggled on my feet to get him all scrunched up and secure. He didn't move.

It would do for the short time it would take to bury his poor mama. The creek sang softly to itself, and I thought she might like to lie near something that sounded so beautiful. Working quickly, I dug a deep hole with a stick next to the creek. I lined the bottom with some grass and picked her up gently by her hands, placing her inside.

Blackie moved to the edge of the grave, but stepped back after I shot him a look. When I was done, I lifted the possum out of my pocket. He didn't seem any worse for the wear. His fur was a little flattened, that's all. I gently placed river rocks on top of the grave.

"I'll make sure your baby is taken care of," I said, looking down at the slight bump in the sand where she lay. "I promise you that." The possum baby nuzzled my hand. Was he hungry? Was he sad? What was I going to do with him? Could he have rabies if he was this little?

Then I had a brainwave. *Mart!*

I took off towards the shade of the big cottonwood trees. The sand beside the water quickly changed to knobs of weeds and craggy stands of Bermuda grass that brushed against my feet as I went. Under the trees, the damp smell of the mossy ground washed over me as I walked.

Mart was my best friend in the whole world. He'd help me. I broke into a trot, pushing past long trailing branches of cottonwood leaves chittering in the breeze. Blackie bounded on past, stopping to smell a big red climbing vine he hadn't peed on yet.

I reached my donkey Jezebel and slid the hand holding the possum up as close to my side as I could, like I didn't even have an arm. Jezebel's ears swiveled back to bear on me, and I switched gears into a slower speed, trying to look as nonthreatening as possible.

I'd begged and begged for a horse. "Every other farm has one," I'd said, and listed the ways a horse would make all our lives easier. But really, I wanted a horse for the same reason I wanted my own dog. Naturally, my dad was against the idea. But when my mama had suggested a donkey—*To keep the coyotes from the calves, dear*—he'd done it. He'd do anything for those cattle. *They* even got the dog—not me!

I'd swallowed my pride and ridden Jezebel since she'd arrived; badly at first and then better as time went on. My dad had initially been against that, too, but had given up after catching me on her for the twenty billionth time. "If she bucks you off or breaks your neck it's your problem," he'd said. I swear she had some sort of magnet in her feet—she could catch me in a red second with a good-placed kick if I wasn't careful. She'd also squashed my foot more times than I could count. For an eleven hand–high midget, she weighed more than an elephant.

She snorted, red-rimmed nostrils flaring as I came in close to her head. I slid the hand that didn't hold my possum real slow towards the nylon rope I'd fixed around the tree. She'd grumble and complain up a storm while you were on her, but leave her alone tied to a tree and she'd stay there the whole day, happily switching her spindly tail back and forth to keep off the flies.

"Now, Jezebel," I said in a warning sort of tone, "I'm gonna get up on you now. I need you to—*Whoa!* Whoa, I said!" Course she'd caught wind of my little possum and went all walleyed crazy on me. I leaped back out of the way as that donkey threw her head up, braying fit to kill. She pulled back on the halter, straining the nylon something fierce. Her eyes rolled wildly as she tugged, her dark gray ears pinned flat to her head. Chunks of grass flew everywhere as she dug in, straining for all she was worth.

I danced from foot to foot as Blackie dove for cover. Jezebel liked him even less than she liked me, mainly because he tried to herd her any time he had a chance. The possum didn't like all the wiggling and let out a weak hiss, which just unhinged the donkey completely. "No!" I yelled, but too late. The metal snap on the halter lead broke with a ringing clang and Jezebel fell, rolling over backwards. I rushed towards her but she was up

in a flash, shaking that big hammerhead of hers and trotting off before I could get close enough to grab her.

Darn it. I couldn't tell you how many lead ropes I'd gone through. I had to pay in *chores* for those things. "Cow!" I yelled after her, but she only flipped her tail at me and broke into a shambling gallop, hitching away towards the gate. Blackie added fuel to the fire, loping after her and nipping at her heels. I felt a fresh surge of anger at them both. I stomped my foot once, but then remembered what I carried. My little possum.

I brought him up to my nose, looking into his little bead eyes as he stared solemnly back at me. His calm calmed me down a little. "Let's get to Mart's, little buddy," I said, and covered him back up. He seemed to agree, curling up into a ball in the base of my palm again. His cold nose pressed into my hand, and it didn't bother me one bit now, just felt right and good.

I knew I'd catch it if I left the darn donkey here. With a sigh, I went over and managed to jerk loose the lead rope. I draped it around my shoulders and headed back towards the gate that led to Mart's, dreaming of beating that donkey black and blue. But I knew I'd never do it.

Chapter 3

It took forever to get over to Mart's if I was coming from my house, but the bottoms were closer. I was crossing land I wasn't supposed to be on. We didn't know who owned it, but I could always apologize if I got found out.

It was the prettiest land you'd ever seen, too: a wide gentle valley with flower-filled sides dropping down to a jumble of oak and crabapple trees at the bottom. Those blended into the big cottonwood trees that stood lining the path of the only major water we had anywhere around us: a wide, shale-bottomed creek, called Skeleton Creek for the bones that had been pulled out of it. "Human bones," some kids whispered, shivering, but I wasn't convinced. Those kids all lived in town and wouldn't know human bones if they came up and bit them in the rear. Half of them had never even seen a real live *cow*.

Hands cupped in front of me, I trotted along the deer trail that took the back way out. The shade came and went as I moved out of the deepest of the bottoms, traveling past the trees, heading up the big hill to the top. The trail got a little treacherous on account of the chunks of blood-red dirt that slid down around my feet, so I had to keep an eye out. Bright red dust swirled up into my nose, tasting like iron.

When I was out and up to the flat top of the canyon rim, I turned to look back while I caught my breath. When that

Oklahoma wind got to whipping the tall, golden grass around, you'd never know there was a bottoms there, much less a creek. It was all hidden. Everything looked okay, no people or anything around to see me and no way to tell I'd been there, so I turned towards the gate and Mart.

Mart was a real doozy of a kid. His dad owned the biggest vet clinic for miles around; he was always giving cattle vaccinations, worming pigs, or chopping off ewe lamb tails. A vet's work was never done out here. But Mart hated all that. He loved computers.

I couldn't understand it. His sister had the most beautiful Appaloosa I'd ever seen, with big, glossy black spots the size of my hand, and he could have had one if he wanted! But no—he squandered the money his grandpa gave him on stupid bits of plastic that hissed together to put words on a glass screen. He was a good kid, though, and had been my best friend ever since I dumped a tray of juices on him in kindergarten because he'd called me a silly girl.

As I neared the gate I could see that sure enough the donkey was standing there straining against the board, eager to get through. She rolled her lip up and shot a look at me, one hind hoof lifting delicately, stopping just short of the ground. The lead clip dangled from her hairy chin like a pendant.

Disgusted, I just glared at her as I went up to the fence. She moved out of the way, but slowly; more of a slide than anything. Her nasty hooves were close to my bare feet, but I reached over and poked her on her flank anyway. Her skin shivered like I was some big fly.

"You idiot," I said, as I held one hand close to my body and fumbled at the gate with the other. "If you were any meaner, I swear. Get out of the way! We're going to Mart's." I slapped her ribs, pushing her aside as I tried to get the gate open one-handed. She crowded me, only backing away when I looped the damaged lead rope through her halter and dug my elbow into her bony chest. She backed up, snorting. Blackie watched everything from the sidelines, bright-eyed, panting up a storm.

As soon as I got the gate open wide enough, Jezebel yanked the rope out of reach and lit off towards home, tail raised over her back like a darned flag.

I was used to this. I just stood there and watched her go. When she got far enough away, she slowed down to a stop and turned to look at me with her long ears perked up. The lead rope looped through her halter slithered down to the ground. I shook my head. She wanted to do things her way, but it didn't necessarily mean that she wanted to be alone when she did it. She needed an *audience*, for crying out loud.

I turned towards Mart's and picked up the lead rope, ignoring her, but when I glanced back I saw her following along behind me, long ears tipped forward, ready to bolt in a red minute if I showed any interest in catching her. Crazy thing.

I rolled my eyes and trotted off, my bare feet sure on the dry ground, over the golden grass, down another canyon gully—and then we were there. Blackie sped past, chasing a rabbit. I called the dog over and looped the lead rope through his collar. He'd done enough damage for one day.

At Mart's I had a quick look around. Nobody was outside. I looked over at the house. It was huge, one of the only two-story houses out here on the plains, and it looked as out of place as an udder on a bull, or so my dad said. It sure was pretty, though. Somehow they'd managed to move large wide slabs of red shale from the bottom of my creek and use it as the outside of the house. No plain brick like ours. The white trim around the huge windows glinted in the sun.

His mom had paid an arm and a leg for what she called "environmental landscaping." I could've done the same thing with some cactus and sage grass, but Mart's grandpa had paid for all of it anyway. He bought Mart's sister her horse, and Mart his computer, too. Something about oil wells.

I looked around the other corner, over where the kitchen was. Roberta wasn't there, either. She was the help that cooked and cleaned and washed and, well, did everything 'round there.

I went to stand under the window of Mart's room. Even in this beautiful weather he'd rather be cooped up inside, pounding away on that keyboard instead of having fun outside. Sometimes I really wondered about him.

I picked up a tiny rock and rolled it in my fingers. Once I'd used too heavy a rock and we'd both been grounded for the resulting broken window, so now I was more careful. I tossed it and heard the clink on the glass. Nothing. I reached down for another rock, but when I looked up there was Mart, leaning out his window, hair mussed and tiny square glasses skewed sideways on his nose.

"P!" he said delightedly, and looked beyond me to the crazy donkey. "What's Jezebel doing behind you? And why's Blackie here?" His eyes goggled at me behind his glasses.

I shrugged. He knew my dad's rule about Blackie just being a herding dog. "I messed up. I have something I need your help with." I lifted the fist I was carrying the possum in, and Mart's eyes sharpened right up as he caught sight of it.

"Be down in a minute." He disappeared from the window.

Chapter 4

"Whatcha got there?"

He'd come scurrying out of the house looking, well, like Mart. Most men—and boys—wore a button-up shirt, short sleeves, with the standard jeans and cowboy belt buckle alongside a pair of dirty old boots. Sometimes even a ball cap. Not Mart. He had on a weird T-shirt with long baggy shorts. Pens in the side pocket of a plaid overshirt rattled. Flip-flops, for crying out loud.

"A possum. See?" My little possum stirred, raising his nose to sniff in Mart's direction. I was pretty sure the reason Mart's eyes widened was because he was secretly falling in love with my new baby. He took a step back, and I wondered if I was right or not.

"A wild animal, P. It could give you rabies. How did you get it?"

I snorted, bringing my hands back to my chest. "He's not a wild animal anymore, Mart; he's just a baby. He doesn't have rabies! Blackie killed his mama." Mart looked down at the dog, who wagged his stub tail at him, panting fiercely.

"You took Blackie into the bottoms? You're lucky your dad isn't here! You'd get tanned!"

"It was a mistake, okay? My mistake. This possum needs my help."

Mart frowned. "What do you think you're gonna do with a baby possum?"

"I'm taking him home with me. Dad is gone, and Mama's not there much. . . . Bet I can keep him hidden until he's old enough to let him go."

I had only one more week of school before it was summer vacation; lots of time then to teach the little guy how to survive on his own. Depending on when Dad came home, that is. Just had to figure out how to keep him hidden till then. It was my civic duty, like my dad had said going to war was for him. And I didn't even have to leave anybody behind or get hurt fighting to do it.

"I don't know, P," Mart said, crossing his arms over his chest. "You know how your dad is."

I needed to convince him. "I've got to help this possum. Can't you help me? Please?"

Mart sighed. "But it's so revolting! It looks like a rat!"

I scowled at him, resisting the urge to put my fingers over the little possum's ears. "He does not! Look at him proper!"

I held him up so that Mart could get a good look at his sweet pointed head with large, shiny black eyes and soft pink nose. His thin gray body with long white guard hairs was all curled up in the bottom of my hand, and his fingers with their tiny claws were still and delicate under his chin as he looked back at Mart. He fit right into my palm; a cuter baby I don't reckon I'd ever seen.

Mart wrinkled his nose and sniffed. "Possum cooties," he muttered.

Time to come to the reason for my visit. "Hey, you know anything about feeding possums?"

He kept staring at the possum. "You don't know how? Don't have a list for it?" Mart always twigged me on my love of making lists.

I rolled my eyes at him. "Mart, do I look like a possum mama? I don't know how old he is, and I don't know if he still needs milk or not. I don't got a list for this. I'm thinking that he needs milk, but . . . I need your innernet help. Can't you help me?"

"It's Internet, P," he said with a snort. "If you want to use it to help you, you might as well say it right." I didn't roll my eyes again, but I was close.

"I'm not here to be best friends with it, Mart. That's what you're here for." I stared at him for a minute and then grinned. He sighed.

"Come on. Let's go look." He turned around and headed for the door, wiping the sweat off his forehead. I took Blackie and tied him in the shade near the water tank, daring to pat his head, even though he ducked away from my hand. "Stay!" I said, trying to act in charge. I could swear the dog rolled his eyes.

I followed Mart inside, whooshing through a blast of cold air. Everything at their house was expensive. The walls were smooth and cool-colored; the floors fancy tile and wood—no carpets for them. The windows throughout the house were long and wide, looking out over the cliff the place perched on. They even had a TV satellite dish. You could get lots of news channels with it to see what was going on in the war. Before my dad got hurt I used to watch it at Mart's 'cause Dad only talked about the camels and the sand in the weekly letter he wrote me—nothing about blood or guns or fighting. He never talked to me and Monica about how he got hurt, either. Since he'd got injured, I didn't have any desire to watch more war stuff.

Ignoring the fancy cast iron rail, I climbed the granite stairs, turned right and then left into Mart's room, looking at the weird poster he had plastered on the door right above the Keep Out sign. Four really hairy guys stood staring out of it, their black hair sticking straight up and the dark makeup on their faces only adding to their gloomy expressions. I'd never ever want to listen to a bunch of folks who looked like they had been playing dress-up in their mama's closet.

I didn't have much call for the kind of music Mart liked, being outside the whole day like I was. Better to listen to the cottonwood trees, the bubbling of the creek, and the music of birds calling to each other.

Mart was already back at his computer, drawn like a magnet, his fingers dancing over the keyboard. We had a computer, but it was Dad's to do taxes on, not a toy for kids.

The light bounced off the painted green walls and into my eyes as I looked down at my possum, nestled in my hand, sleeping. His sides fluttered up and down as he lay there so still. Mart typed away, clickety-clackety, and I let my mind wander.

What to name him? I really missed my dad, but I didn't like the idea of calling a possum after him. My gran already had somebody named after her—me, and who ever heard of a possum being called Princess? Besides, I didn't like my name, which is why I made everybody call me P.

But my gramps . . . I narrowed my eyes. His name had been Eisenhower. His first name, I mean, had been Eisenhower. It had been funny to hear him and my gran talk about when they met. Eisenhower and Princess. Could you get crazier names? My gramps had always gone by Ike. *Ike!* Now that was something. . . . And he was even dead, so he wouldn't mind. . . . I rolled it over my tongue, looking at my little friend as he flipped onto his side. Ike sounded good. It was short and sweet. And I didn't have any better ideas. Ike it was.

I looked back up at Mart. "Found anything?"

"You betcha." He turned around on his stool to look at me with his eyes sparkling, a little troll hunched over in his information cave.

Chapter 5

Mart leaned back in his chair. The sparkle hadn't left his eyes, but he looked to be thinking for a minute. "Okay, P. Stay here. I'll be right back." Without explaining, he jumped out of his chair and left the room. I listened to his feet flip-flopping down the stairs and started at the sound of the front door slamming. What in the world was he doing? I went to look out his window and watched him hurry across the driveway and disappear inside the barn.

The machine on his desk made a gunshot kind of sound and I whirled around to look at it. It didn't do anything else, just sat and clicked and whirred to itself like a really big wristwatch. Ike had jerked up at the noise but settled down again.

I looked around Mart's room. There were papers everywhere and lots of little plastic superhero figures perched among them. Stickers of robots and empty video-game cases decorated the top of the monitor. Our school yearbook lay on the desk next to the computer, open to the page with the moonlight-and-magnolias picture of Miss Cassie Knight. She'd signed it for him, like she was a rock star: "Hi," it said. The top of the *i* was a big fat heart. Her bug eyes stared up out of the picture. She was the most popular girl in school, but popular didn't mean nice, and all the girls knew she had a mean streak. The boys never figured it out.

Cassie rode our bus, the farm route, to school. Her dad was big in cows; he'd managed to make himself quite a few enemies around the county by buying up all the land going begging and sticking his cattle on it instead of farming it, like he ought. They were great big lumpy cows, too. Not fancy like my dad's—just cow mutts. Hamburger.

The door opened and I whipped around, trying not to look like I was nosing in his stuff. Mart went tomato red. Looking anywhere but at the yearbook, he held up a jar of white powder and a cup.

"What's that?"

He cracked open the top, letting me sniff it. It whooshed into my nose, a strong rich smell that made my mouth water.

"Cow milk replacer," he said, screwing the top back on and setting it down on the bed. "See?" He dumped some of the dry milk into the cup which was filled with water, and stirred it, watching the water go milky as the powder dissolved. Ike shifted in my palm as the warm smell of rich milk drifted our way. It smelled pretty good, I had to say. My stomach growled.

Mart dipped the spoon in and then held it out to the little possum, who at first didn't seem to know what to do, although he sure seemed to like the smell of that milk. He sniffed and sniffed, standing and walking to the end of my hand, straining towards it. He stuck his tongue in the milk, sneezed once, and started lapping it up. His little pink fingers clenched my hand as he leaned, so Mart motioned for me to take the spoon and get it closer to him.

I took it. He was really slurping now.

I looked up to see Mart smiling, his blue eyes lighting up his face. "There. You'll need to give it to him for a while," he said. "I couldn't find any data on the approximate size and weight the opossum should be when he is weaned. Let's just say that he should have it for the foreseeable future. I'll get some information together on what adult possums eat and have a list for you on Monday."

We watched the little possum eagerly gulping in the milk until he seemed to be full. He stopped drinking, at last, and laid back down on my hand. He burped and licked his lips, and we giggled.

"Now comes the gross part," Mart said, and took the spoon and cup away. He walked back over to the computer and did something with the mouse. The screen changed color and there were some pictures I couldn't make out.

"What?"

He swiveled around on his chair and grinned at me. I didn't like his look—not one bit. "He has to go to the bathroom."

"Do I need to take him outside or something for that?"

"Nope. You've got to massage his rear end."

I blinked. "I have to *what*?"

Mart strolled over and put his hands on his hips. He was laughing now. "You've got to massage his stomach and his rear to get him to go to the bathroom." He snorted, then rummaged in his dresser drawer and pulled out a sock. I stared at him in horror as he held it out to me, waiting. His shoulders kept jerking around and I knew he was still laughing. "With this. You can use toilet paper or paper towels at home."

"You're kidding me."

"Nope." He walked back over to the computer and, bending down, quoted, " 'The orphan opossum must be massaged on the stomach and rectum after eating or drinking, until the movement has fully passed.' "

"Movement?"

"His poo. And pee."

This didn't sound good.

Mart's eyes sparkled when he looked back at me, and I knew he was paying me back for seeing his dream girl autograph.

"You want me to make my possum go to the bathroom? With my finger?" He nodded, and I took a deep breath. "I don't know about this. Why do I need to do it?"

"P, you have to. He can't do it when he's so little. He'll explode. The web page says they can't use the muscles of their intestines until later, when they're bigger."

Not knowing precisely how to massage a possum belly, I took the sock from Mart and flipped Ike over on his back. He accepted it, lazing about on my slightly shaking hand as I surveyed his stomach. White frosty hair moved up and down softly as he breathed, and I shook my head. "I can't believe I'm going to do this." I stuck my finger into the sock, put it against his stomach, and closed my eyes.

"Open your eyes."

"Come on." But I did. And Ike looked to be a boy.

"I think you need to rub harder."

"Look, do you want to do this?"

"Nope. I just do the research, remember?" Mart smirked.

"Be quiet." Would he ever *go*? I rubbed his belly gingerly, moving it back towards his rear as I waited for something to happen.

Then it did, with a popping sound.

"Gross!"

"Man, I didn't know a little thing like that could go on for so long." Mart was staring down in fascination at Ike. The little possum twisted onto his other side and curled up, happy as a clam. I slowly lifted the stinking bundle of sock. I *really* needed to wash my hands.

"Come on," said Mart. "Let's get you to your place."

The aching rumble in my belly seconded his plan, and I followed at a trot. It was past time for lunch and I wouldn't get any at Mart's house. We scooted down the stairs, Mart hopping and me right behind him, nearly bumping into him as he shoved his feet into some sneakers by the door. The cold inside gave way to the heat wall that was an Oklahoma summer.

Mart headed for the barn, and the powerful whine of the four-wheeler stirred to life inside. I untied Blackie, who just stood there, ears pinned back and growling. He hated that thing, and although I wasn't crazy about the noise either, it sure got you places fast. Walking, it took me a good twenty-five minutes to get to Mart's, but riding only ten or so. Even with Mart driving.

The barn door whooshed aside and Mart drove out, rumbling past the algae-filled cattle tank full of goldfish and the pipe corrals that were the vet clinic holding pens, then slowing up about fifteen feet away from me. He had his helmet and pads and jacket on. Mart didn't go any faster than a bare crawl, but he was always careful. He flipped his visor back.

"What about the donkey? And Blackie?" he asked, fingers paused over the gas switch.

I looked at Jezebel, ears up and focused on me. She snorted. "Aw, just let her find her own way home. I'm mad at her anyways." Nobody was crazy enough to steal the old biddy. Her reputation preceded her, as my dad said.

Blackie'd follow, even though if he had any marbles he'd know I'd stick him back in his kennel when we got home. It was almost time for Mama to get there, if she wasn't already.

I climbed carefully onto the wide plastic seat behind Mart, settling firmly in. I rolled my possum up in my shirt like a little possum burrito and stuck a hand over him to keep him stable. He didn't mind at all.

I was pretty pleased with myself so far. Now all I had to do was figure out how to take him to school. And get him past my mama and sister.

Chapter 6

It didn't look like anybody was home as we drove in, horn honking and lights flashing.

Mart crept up the driveway and parked, pulling off his helmet as he climbed off onto the cement. I exited the back a little more slowly, wiping bugs off my face. "Be right back."

He nodded as I locked Blackie in his kennel and made sure he had plenty of water. Then I ran over to the mailbox. Maybe we had Dad Mail! I shut my eyes a minute, crossing my fingers. Usually Dad wrote once a week, and it was about time for us to get a big packet. His being so far away at the war and hurt, he said, made him want to write us on paper, one letter for each. Plus I knew from listening in on his phone conversations with Mama that he figured if anything ever happened to him, we'd have the letters. I didn't want to think about that.

The mailbox squeaked a protest as I cracked it, then flung it open wide with a big grin. We did have mail! There it was—the fat manila envelope from Dad.

I nearly danced a happy dance right there, but remembered my possum. Instead I pulled the envelope out and clasped it to my chest before sticking it down the front of my shorts for safe-keeping. I left the rest of the mail to sit there. It was just bills.

I headed back across the yard and listened outside the house a minute for the telltale pulse of Mon's music. Nothing to be heard, not even a sneeze, and I sighed with relief. "Monica's not here," I said to Mart. "Come on." Our house wasn't anything much, but my dad had built it from scratch with some friends back when he and Mama were first married. It was long and low and the colors of the Oklahoma plains—golds and reds and browns—with a gently sloped dark bay roof. When you walked through the garage the rule was to take off your shoes, but I didn't wear them and so didn't have any to take off. Mart struggled with his sneakers, dragging them off by the heels.

We didn't use our air-conditioning as much as Mart's parents, so you couldn't really tell you were inside. But my house was friendly and cheerful. You could sit down without worrying you were going to break something—and Mart swore the food in the fridge was always better than anything Roberta made at his house, so I guess it wasn't all bad.

I'd thought about what to do with my little friend on the ride over. If I was going to take him to school, I'd need something foolproof to hide him in. A purse would give me away right from the start.

"I'll be right back. Make yourself at home, Mart," I said as I headed down the hall. I heard a shout of agreement behind me and didn't pay him any more mind. He'd take care of lunch while I solved my big problem.

It had to be a pretty secret way to carry him, I thought as I walked to my bedroom. I pushed the door open and glanced around for inspiration. Horse posters stared back, and my eyes ping-ponged off the messy dresser, the overflowing clothes hamper, my cowboy hat, and the rest of the general destruction that was the state of my room on any given day. There were books everywhere, too, but nothing I could carry a possum in.

I pulled the envelope out of my shorts, set it down gently on my bed, and kissed my possum on his head in delight. A letter!

First the carry thing. I looked around. It had to be something like a pouch necklace or something, but bigger. . . . Maybe a list *would* help me get organized.

My dad was real organized, too. When he'd gone to war and left me in charge of the farm, he'd given me a book with blank paper on the inside and pictures of a horse on the outside. *It's for your farm responsibilities, Princess,* Mama'd said.

You'll need it to keep track of your chores for me while I'm gone. And it'll help you with your spelling, Dad added. I had a problem with silent consonants.

I'd named it my Lookbook. I put his letters in it too, and I liked that I could have everything special in one place. It got to where I felt like I was missing a leg when I didn't have it on me, but the bottoms were no place for a Lookbook. I fished it out from underneath my pillow and wrote down:

1. *Sok*
2. *Purse (Mama's?)*
3. *Bakpak*
4. *Jeans poket*
5. . . . . *??*

I sighed a little and put the pencil down. What else could carry a possum? Big enough for his tail to fit too? I pulled him out of the T-shirt sausage he'd ridden over in and looked at him. His long tail dangled gently off the edge of my hand, and he made a pretty good sized lump where he lay. I couldn't put him in my jeans pocket; I'd squish him.

Monica? Would she have something I could use? I looked at the white wall, slitting my eyes to concentrate better. There *was* . . .

Years ago my sister had "blossomed," as Mama called it. Actually, we'd both had to sit through a conversation where my mama's talk of *birds* and *bees* and *flowering* had reduced me to a red-faced mess. After she'd got the talk "out of the way forever, thank goodness!" she'd taken Mon out to the mall, where they'd bought her sports bras and new underwear.

But those sports bras were perfect! With a little bit of string underneath them and some tape on the sides to hold them down . . .

When I pushed open the door to Mon's room, pink and white hit me like a blast in the face, and I glanced down at my dirty toes resting at the edge of her pristine carpet. I stopped cold. She'd know if I went in there with my dirty feet.

I ran to my room, shoved my feet into some sneakers, and ran back, checking the bottoms as I paused at the doorway. Clear.

I snuck in, tiptoeing past the frilly bed with its angel and cupid cover, past the white dresser with its gold edges. I made it to the small dresser under the window. I looked behind me just to check and sure enough, not a footprint—nothing to tell I'd been there.

Feeling pretty good about my spy skills, I pulled open the top drawer and reached in, rifling through prescription inhalers, lipstick Mama had given her—pink; her prom flower corsage—dead; her newest boyfriend's picture—ugly. I moved down to the "undergarments," as my mama called them, and pulled one up.

Then another.

I was a little astounded, truth be told. They came in *colors*? They were all cotton and looked like miniature straightjackets. I grabbed a white one. Then I shoved everything back in as neatly as I could and gently put the replacement inhalers back on top, where she'd left them. All set.

"Eat!" Mart yelled, and I jumped a mile straight up. Whipping around, I made for the door, kicking off the sneakers into the open mess of my room and slamming my door shut behind me. I raced back to the kitchen, possum secure in one hand and bra in the other. The strong tomato smell of lasagna wafted around the corner as I ran into the kitchen.

Mart looked up from cutting slices as I triumphantly brandished the bra above my head like a football fan gone loco. He blinked at me, then at what I was twirling around, and licked the spoon. He slid a plate in front of me and took a seat across, cutting big wedges in his piece to cool it as he stared at me.

"What've you got?"

"A bra!"

Mart blushed. "A . . . bra?"

"I'll explain." And I did.

He still didn't look too convinced as he went for another helping. Ike lay curled up in my lap, snoring away. As I finished eating I looked out the window. I knew Monica might be home any moment now, no time to waste.

"Okay, Mart, I'm going to need your help. Hold on to this possum." I held out Ike but had to get after Mart a little more before he'd take him. He kept muttering about rabies.

I shucked off my shirt and grabbed the sports bra, wriggling it over my head. As I pulled it on, I noticed Mart looking away, chewing furiously and turning the shade of a rotten tomato. I tugged the sports bra down and faced to him.

"What's your problem?"

"Well . . . I . . . uh . . ."

I hooked my finger in the top and pulled it out a little.

"Shoot, it's too big." I grabbed some string and cut off a longish piece, then wrapped it securely around the bottom of the bra where it met my chest. I paused to check the effect. And wiggled. When I pulled it out some it held okay. Straight up against my chest, like I'd planned. I turned around to find Mart staring at me, looking horrified.

Chapter 7

"What?" I didn't have a booger, did I? I reached up to check.

"You just *changed* in front of me. I just saw your *chest*." With every word he got redder, and holding little Ike in front of him like a barrier between us. I could feel the heat of his face from where I stood.

"So?" I looked down. "Not much to see. And you are my best friend, right?"

"Well, yeah." He didn't meet my eyes. He was so red it was almost criminal.

"Oh, enough already. Give me Ike." He seemed okay—sleeping, his belly still puffed up from his lunch at Mart's. Turning away with a snort at Mart, I carefully lifted my shirt and deposited Ike inside the sports bra, where he twisted around a little but fell back into a snoring heap. He was nice and dry now, and he wasn't at all stinky or anything. I prodded the outside of my shirt, but everything looked normal. My experiment was a success! I turned back to Mart with a grin. He seemed to have faded his way back to normal. He eyed my front but didn't say anything. After a moment, he reached for more lasagna.

"You said something about rabies. Is your dad finding lots of animals with rabies?"

He nodded as he cut out another slice and slid it onto his plate.

"Old Man Longer had to shoot a horse. She was drooling something fierce and walking funny. Dad took some of her brain—"

"Ew!" I motioned towards the food. "Come on, we're eating here!"

"Sorry." But he wasn't, and took a bite before continuing. "Anyway, Dad had it tested, and sure enough. He's worried there's some live animals out there that might have it." He took a drink of water and set it down, looking at the glass. "You being careful?"

I snorted and rolled my eyes. "Duh."

He relaxed, cut up some more bites, and waited for them to cool down. After eating practically all my mama's lasagna, he left. I put the sad remains of the lasagna in the fridge for Mon, and the plates on the side of the sink for her to clean up. Dishes were inside work—not mine.

The letter pushed to the front of my brain. Could I wait until I gave the packet to Mama to get mine? I looked down at the possum. Ike slept quietly. He'd not made a peep since his bathroom break. Nope. I knew I couldn't. I turned and headed for my room. Once there I picked up the envelope, looking at the stamps. I got the unusual stamps; whole pages in my Lookbook were taken up with camels and suns and pictures of old guys with lines crossed through them, as well as old air mail stamps. There was a stamp on this envelope I hadn't seen; I marked it in my mind, so I would make sure to grab it after Mama was done.

With only the slightest guilty feeling, I opened the envelope and rifled through. My letter wasn't very thick and I tried not to frown. I unfolded it slowly, the thin-lined yellow paper crackling. I could see Dad's writing, and it made me smile. His handwriting was ugly and small, like mine. He didn't mess around either, just came right to the point.

P:

How are the cattle? Did the bull come back yet? How about the garden, are you keeping up on weeding the lettuce? You know your mama likes that. Has Joe been taking

Blackie to train him on cows? Make sure and let me know. How's the wheat coming along? Does Joe plan on harvesting it first? Do you know?

I looked up. Nope, I didn't know. Nothing had changed in his letters, at least. They were always about the farm. I guilty-wiggled on the bed a little when I read the part about Blackie. I hadn't checked with Joe about any of that stuff. I'd forgotten. I went on reading.

It's been real hot here, and the sunsets are real nice. Not as nice as the sunsets over the farm, but they'll do. I've picked up some good farming advice from another soldier that's rooming with me. I'm sending you some pictures one of the other soldiers made of the camels. Did you know they farm them just like we do cows?
Your spelling is getting lots better. Keep working on it.
Dad

That was it. Farm and sand. I folded the letter carefully before reaching for the Lookbook and sticking it inside. There weren't that many in there; even though he'd been gone a long time, almost a year, he'd only started writing the letters recently—right around the time he'd stopped wanting to talk to us by phone. Right around the time he'd gotten hurt.

Didn't matter. For now, he was okay. I got up and headed to Blackie's kennel. When I got there he looked at me and his ears pricked up.

"Come on, boy." He jumped to his feet.

Time for his training.

He was the cattle dog, and Dad was real strict about him being in the kennel when he wasn't working. Blackie listened to whoever the boss was, and now that Dad was gone, I'd been trying to make him listen to me. But it was harder than I thought. So I'd decided to do things the old-fashioned way: food.

"Sit, Blackie."

The dog just looked up at me, panting, and tipped his head to the side. I swallowed my irritation and checked that the possum was still up against my chest.

"Come on, Blackie! Sit. *Sit*." I waved a crusty piece of lasagne at him, and his eyes glittered as he grabbed it from me in one gulp. Now he'd sit! Or maybe not. I watched as he swallowed, and then his teeth flashed as he dug into his side to chase a flea. I rolled my eyes. I couldn't even get him to listen to me for food. How could I ever get him to be my friend if he didn't pay attention to me at all?

It was getting dark. I had chores to do, so he needed to go back to his kennel. "Come on, dog." He came. *Then*.

Blackie didn't seem to have any issues with the kennel, and he jumped inside without a whimper. He headed for his doghouse and flopped down. I went over to the can on the outside and opened it, dug up a good half bucket of food, and poured it into his bowl. He'd already gone to sleep, probably dreaming of eating possums, darn it. He still had blood around his mouth.

Cows were next on my chore list. I counted the cattle and made sure they were all standing and not sick, and wrote it all down in the Lookbook. Additional chores were to go into the chicken house and get the eggs, which was not always as much fun as you might think.

I was pretty happy with my possum carrier invention as I jogged along. Ike was warm but still, and my hands were free so I could open the corral gates. My dad had made our corrals and lots of individual pens. Six-foot-high iron fences opened one pen into another like a honeycomb to get into the big huge pasture where the cows were.

I trotted past the meat steer, then climbed to the top of the fence to check his food. You had to really lean over to look at the level of corn in his feeder. He wasn't very friendly, but then again he didn't have much of a life. The plan was to get him as fat as possible by winter and then make him our meat for the following year. I always felt a little uncertain as to how to address my future hamburger, so I just made sure he had food and left. He didn't seem to mind.

The cattle were close this evening, and I was happy about that. Normally I didn't mind going out to the farthest reaches of the pasture, but today I was worried that Ike would get hungry again, and I wanted to make sure I was near home. The long grass twitched against my bare legs as I went around and through the tall clumps. Nothing much stirred in the late afternoon. The cicadas had started to whir. Bugs flew up and around me as I walked past. For as far as my eye could see, everything was f-l-a-t. The only things that stuck up out of the limitless horizon were a couple trees, one or two houses, and some cows. I knew the creek was there, but you sure couldn't see it.

Could Dad see so far, where he was? I sighed and started walking again. When the cows came into view, I stopped. I was close enough.

My dad's precious cattle, some lying down, some standing, were all chewing their cud. I never got the cow thing. They were a fancy French type, Charolais. Pretty, don't get me wrong, all shimmery white and glossy. But they were still just cows. Dad had them brought from far away, like Canada or something, and had gloated over them every night since they'd arrived, like a pirate with his treasure. "They're our future, P." He'd look at them, and his eyes would get all soft. "Soon we'll have a huge herd and people will come to us for Charolais." But Dad worked at the bank and only did farm stuff at night, so I didn't know how they could be our future.

I reached in my backpack and pulled out the Lookbook. Everybody was there. I'd named them all, seeing as we only had six and a bull. The bull was visiting some other cows and was gone right now. The six had babies that'd been born earlier in the spring. Mart's dad had been the one to birth them all, and man were the little calves cute. Their liquid brown eyes followed my movements, and they skittered around with their tails in the air as I circled the herd, checking on everyone. I opened up the Lookbook to the next blank page, the one right past my newest letter, wrote the date, and then:

1. Loosygoosy: ok. Lots of flies on her leg. (chek)

I walked up as close as I dared to see why there were so many flies. They were the best indicator of something wrong out here, and sure enough, she had a couple of crusty cuts. She was jumpy, too, and moved out of my way when I tried to get closer. That in itself wasn't normal for her. She was usually the friendliest one and let me pet her.

She wasn't limping too bad, so I shrugged and wrote it down. If she was worse tomorrow and the next day, I'd call Mart's dad. I'd make sure to mention it to Dad in my next letter.

2. Chaka: ok.
3. Buffy: ok. Kind of Skinny.
4. Rocky: ok.
5. Gimp: ok.
6. Gidget: ok.
7. Beelzebub: gone.
8. Calfes: ok.
Grass: Its dry. Fences good. No rabid animals.

All the calves wouldn't make one cow, so they were lumped together under one number.

Putting the Lookbook in my backpack, I felt my shirt for my little possum. He nuzzled my hand.

I'd have to hurry if I wanted to take care of the chickens before Mama got home. I ran as fast as I could back to the corrals, one hand against my chest. Jezebel was against the corral gate and braying her head off, so I let her in and she made for the high pasture, bucking through the corrals just for good measure.

The chicken house was right outside the entrance of the main corral. I put my backpack down, picked some handfuls of long Bermuda grass, and pushed open the creaky wooden door of the henhouse. "Hey, girls!" I called as I went inside the building, shutting the door behind me and scattering the grass on the floor. "Chi-i-ick! Chi-i-ick! Chi-i-ick!"

Suspicious clucks and "brr-oaks" broke the silence. What light there was sifted through thick plastic laid over the windows. The feather tufts floated in the sunlight shining through the plastic, making the place look like it was glowing.

I stopped and looked over to my right. The nesting boxes covered one whole wall of the long enclosed space, set on top of each other two stories deep. Beady eyes glared at me from the dark entryways. I picked up the heavy stick leaning against the wire window and walked forward. I'd had far too many pecking attacks from mad old-biddy hens that were going to protect their freshly laid eggs, so I didn't even bother now, just poked them until they got out of the way. Enraged squeaks and squawks followed my progress as I made my way down the row.

I didn't have anything official like an egg basket to put the eggs in. Usually I just doubled up my T-shirt and lumped them all in there. I'd tried using my backpack once and dropped it. After I had to clean that thing out, I didn't use my backpack anymore.

My little possum was still sleeping peacefully as I started collecting eggs. As I reached up, straining to get the eggs from the second row, I thought about his food. I *could* take a soda bottle full in my backpack. I knew my sister hid some sodas in her room. I'd just borrow one and clean the bottle out real good.

I poked a chicken out of the way and took her eggs.

I'd go to the bathroom when I needed to feed him. That would work okay.

I would need to make a list for school.

I stuck my hand up into the next box. It was empty. I didn't get what was happening for a minute. Instead of the round blobs of eggs, my fingers touched a long, cool, rubbery thing. My stomach fell about four stories below my feet, and sweat broke out over my nose. I knew that feeling.

Chapter 8

"Eee! Snake! *Snake!*"

I busted out of that henhouse like my tail was on fire, scattering eggs like bird shot. I don't know how Ike managed to stay asleep, the way I was screaming like a banshee. Each egg cracked into a wet splat near my feet as I hopped around, screeching and hollering. I wiped my hand on anything that would take the slimy feeling away, but no dice. My skin was crawling like it was covered in boogers.

"Eee!"

"What in the world are you doing, Princess?" I jumped about a mile higher than I was already. Ike finally woke up and dug his claws in. Blackie ran around me, barking.

Wait. Blackie, out? *Oh.* Joe was there.

"Joe, there's a *snake* in there!" I said, taking one long, shuddering breath after another. My skin kept wrinkling up and moving around over the top of my muscles like I was shedding it or something, and my hand tingled. I tried to hold it still, just to check I hadn't been bitten.

My dad's best friend looked at me and then at the building, where not a cluck emerged. He raised an eyebrow. "Well, then." He spit a long stream of brown liquid onto the ground, and I almost heaved. "Ought I ta shoot it?" The man loved his bird-shot gun. He carried it with him everywhere, its sleek black length adding a long exclamation point to anything he said.

"What? No!" The last time he'd used his gun in the hen-house, we didn't have any eggs for a week, and Mama had jumped on my case for his craziness. Dad said he should've volunteered for the National Guard, the way he liked to throw that gun around, and I was inclined to agree with him.

Joe's weathered face cracked into a grin. "No gunnin'? Well, then. You got a rake?"

Did I ever.

I hurried over to the toolshed and brought him one with a nice long handle. He spit again, (I always had to watch where I stepped after he'd come by the farm) and hefted the rake in his hand. He set his gun down gently, then jerked his head towards the door. "Open it."

I backed away, put my hands behind me for good measure,

and shook my head. *Forget it.* My skin was still crawling. "No way. *You* do it."

He pushed his stained cowboy hat back off his forehead and scratched his grizzled hair. Flakes drifted down and were whirled away by the wind. Blackie looked from one to the other of us, eyes shining. "Awright." He settled the rake a little better in his hand as I watched him mosey over to the door. His blue plaid shirt was ripped in the back, and its long tail dangled out above his jeans. Scuffed boots kicked against the gravel of the drive, scattering it as he went over to the door, opened it, and went inside. He was about the slowest-moving thing I had ever been around.

A commotion started up in the henhouse. The chickens were going nuts—lots of thumps and noises accompanied by hysterical cackling. I tensed up, waiting. Sometimes the snake made a break for it.

The door flung open, and Joe stood there with his potbelly supporting his arms, which supported the rake and—yup, a black snake. A big chopped-up one. My stomach dropped another notch and I swallowed hard.

"Pretty big'un," he said, walking out and leaving me to shut the door. I shivered but ran up behind him, securely latching the wooden door before walking around his side to stare at the snake. It must have been almost as long as I was tall, and rail thin, except for lumps—my eggs, darn it!—all down its bloody surface. It was definitely dead, though. Its mouth gaped open, long tongue dangling out of an almost completely severed head.

Drops of dark blood followed Joe as he walked over and slung the snake into the high weeds behind the chicken house. It made a sick crashing sound as it fell to the ground, and I rubbed my arms, trying to force the goose bumps down. "Thanks."

Joe finished wiping the rake off in the grass and propped it up against the wall. He walked back over real slow and picked up his gun, sighting down the barrel. I bet he was wishing he could've used it. "Nodda problem. Have you checked on the cows?"

He talked slow, too. Everything had an extra vowel, a "yuh" sound. So it sounded like "Ha-yuv you che-yucked o-un the cao-yus?"

"Yeah."

"Good. I'll be bringing Beelzebub back next coupla days. Oh, and I'm takin' Blackie with me. Got some hefty cow work I gotta do tomorrow."

I just nodded. At least Dad'd be happy Blackie was keeping his skills up. I looked over at the dog. "Blackie, come." Miracle of miracles, he did and stood in front of me.

"Sit."

He stared up at me, and I could almost hear him decide to ignore me. He stayed standing.

"*Sit*, Blackie."

Nothing doing.

"Sit, dawg." Joe didn't even look down at him, and darn if Blackie didn't plunk his rear end down, looking up at Joe with devotion in his eyes.

Man, that chapped my hide.

"Everything else around here awright?"

"Yeah."

He'd promised my dad that he'd check on us while he was gone and he did—about every week or so. He'd time it real exact, too. He'd push it out until it was dinnertime and we had to feed him. The man ate like a mule; almost as much as me, and that was saying something. I couldn't blame him too much, though. I wouldn't want to eat at his house either. His wife could burn water.

I had a problem with him showing up even once a week, if I was honest with myself. *I* was in charge of the farm. Just because he was a grown-up and checked on us every once in a while, he got all the credit.

"I don't think you need to be doing your explorations down at the crick right now, P," he said.

"I can so." I said it without even thinking. He couldn't boss me around; it wasn't like he was my dad or anything.

He snorted. "You know what I've done lately?" He spread his legs out a little and braced them. The wind whipped the strands of hair around his face, and his stinky body odor got in my nose.

I shrugged. "Nope."

"I've done shot three raccoons on our land, so far gone with the rabies they could hardly move. I've done kilt a badger and a fox, what I haven't seen around in a donkey's age, who came right at me, drooling something fierce." He bent over a little and looked directly in my eyes. "I'd sure hate to see you get bit and get the rabies. Them shots hurt, you know. Dyin' from rabies is even worse."

I shook my head. "Joe, I'm careful."

"See that you are." He paused. "Your mama keeping up all right?"

I relaxed a little. "Yeah."

He got real still and looked up. "Hold your ears."

"What? Why?"

He suddenly raised the gun and sighted into the blue, pulling the trigger. I jumped and the possum freaked out, hissing and crawling everywhere as I gasped and tugged at the front of my shirt. I probably looked like a crazy person.

A goose came plummeting down from the sky, landing with a fat splat in front of me. It was dead, dead, dead, and I got mad. Blackie didn't even twitch from his sit but stretched his nose out, sniffing.

"What'd you go and do that for? You can't do that here! No guns!" I yelled.

Joe looked a little taken aback. "Princess. Was just a goose." He glanced at the dead bird, but I was past caring.

"I don't like your gun! This is our land!" I was still wiggling around, struggling with my shirt. Ike was going nuts in there. His hair was poofed out and he was trembling, and he hissed again, almost chittering in fear. He was flat out having a meltdown. I'd have to go into the house.

Joe frowned. "What's that noise?"

"I gotta go!"

"Why for?" he called out as I made for the house. The craziness of the situation made me almost laugh out loud as I ran.

"You just scared the poo out of me!" I screeched.

I heard him snort and shout out, "Be careful!" I waved and kept on, rounding the barn side and going straight into the kitchen and then my room. I pulled out the possum and stared at him, amazed. His poor little eyes were wide and all black, and he shivered—a fine continuous tremor kept running through him from the front of his head down to his tail and back up again. His hair was still all poofy. He hissed at me, so upset and scared I almost wanted to cry. I could hardly blame him. How would I get him to calm down? What calmed me down when I was upset? Food.

I grabbed the bottle and fumbled it open. The smell seemed to relax him straightaway, and I slumped in relief. He drank one more spoon than he had at Mart's, and I decided I would keep a list of how much he ate.

By the time he finished eating, he'd stopped shivering, although his feet still clenched tightly into my hand. Poor thing. He really didn't like guns.

Chapter 9

I wrinkled my nose and did his toilet. The way he ate, I'd need to find some toilet paper or some paper towels and keep them on me all the time. It was too gross to use a sock. How would I keep the poo smell away after I used it? It would need to be something I could close and hide in the trash.

Mama had zip-top bags she used for freezing stuff. They would work. Nobody was home yet, so I snuck out to the kitchen, possum in hand, and took about half the box. Back in my room, I stuffed the sock in one of them and zipped it closed. And sniffed. Nothing.

I put Ike back in my shirt.

After I'd hidden the rest of the bags in my sock drawer, I got out the Lookbook. I'd decided to keep all Ike's info at the back, in his own section. A hidden part. I shuffled the pages around, leafing slowly past my dad's letters and the farm reports till I found a nice blank page. Then I wrote:

1. Mart's (start) 4 tabelspoons
2. 5 tabelspoons

I paused a moment. What else had I wanted to write? Oh right, school. I drew a line across the page and made a list of things I'd need to take with me on Monday.

1. *Milk botel (milk)*
2. *Zip-top bag plus old sok*
3. *Spoon*

I inspected him as he snored peacefully. It was pretty great that he was taking to being adopted so well. Except that gun thing. I would have to watch that.

I heard the door slam and threw the blanket on my bed over him, running ponies and clouds hiding the small body. I grabbed her letter and met my sister at the hall entryway.

At sixteen, Monica was short, pudgy, and the dark to my light. Her brown hair stood neatly in its hair clasp, and her brown eyes narrowed at me suspiciously as I stood, trying to act all nonchalant. Then she sneezed, and I blanched. A possum allergy and the gig was up.

"What are you doing inside, Princess?" My eyebrows went down as I glared at her. She *knew* I didn't like that name, she *knew* I preferred P, but she liked to mess with me. She flounced past me, hideous pink outfit clashing with just about everything. She reeked of perfume and I tried to breathe through my mouth.

"Dad wrote." I said, holding out her letter. She reached for it and I continued, "Besides, can't a body be inside sometimes?" I leaned against the side of the door as she took her letter, opening it. It was shorter than mine, I saw.

She shoved the letter into her purse and opened the door to her room. I tensed up a little. With her evil powers, could she tell I'd been in there?

Her bra seemed to contract around me. She shot me a glance as she slung her purse onto her bed, then opened her dresser drawer and rummaged around. I could hardly breathe. Big fat drops of sweat rolled down between my shoulders. She pulled a new inhaler out and took a whiff, huffing slightly. Her hands shuffled through her clothes, messing them up even more than they had been, and I relaxed. Scot-free this time, at least.

"Not when the body is *you*. Can't you stop talking like that?

I feel like I'm in *The Beverly Hillbillies,* you hick. And unless you want to help me clean and warm up supper, I suggest you make yourself scarce until Mother gets home."

"I don't talk like a hick. Dad talks this way."

She rolled her eyes. "*Your* dad does."

It hurt my feelings when she talked like that.

The phone rang and Mon dove for it, but I got to it first. I slipped her a smile as I pressed the button.

"Hello?"

"Fishstick!"

"Gran!" I grinned and Mon rolled her eyes, flouncing out the door. Gran'd always called me Fishstick. Evidently when I was little all I'd eat were fish sticks. It was her way of giving me a hug.

"How are you?" I walked into my room and shut the door.

"Good, child, good. Your mama there?"

"No, Gran, not yet. Any time though."

She sighed. "You doing good, Fishstick?"

I lifted the corner of the blanket and smiled at my possum, lying full out and snoring away. I put the cover back down. "Pretty good, Gran. When you coming to visit?"

She laughed, deep and rich. "That's why I'm calling. I reckon I'll be there in four weeks or so, stay a couple weeks. That sound good?"

"Sounds good," I said, laughing weakly.

Shoot. I was pretty confident about hiding Ike from Mon. Even Mama. But not Gran. She had eyes like a hawk. She'd catch me faster than a duck could jump on a june bug.

"You hear anything from your dad? What else is going on there?"

"We got a packet today. There was a new stamp." Gran was real impressed with my stamp collection. "Other than that, not much, though there's lots of rabies going around here. Joe said—"

"Joe? That scruffy old fart still around?"

That's why I loved my gran. She tells it like it is. When I stopped laughing, I said, "Yeah, he comes to get Blackie a lot and then he comes by to look at the farm and get a free meal every once in a while, too."

"Not while I'm there," she said, almost under her breath. "Will you tell your mama I called?"

"Will do, Gran. Talk to you soon?"

"Sure thing, Fishstick. Love you, honey."

"Love you, too, Gran."

The click in my ear sounded lonely as I pulled the phone away. I got Ike, tucking him gently inside my shirt, and left the house.

I sat down on the front porch to wait for Mama and watched the sun go down. This used to be the time I'd be following my dad around. Ever since he'd been gone, I'd liked this part of the day the least. I stared into the sun. The brilliant red spread through my eyes, washing out the other colors until all I could see was blood.

Was it as hot there in the war as it was here? When Dad first got there he seemed okay, but then, he just . . . ran out of things to say. His voice would get all scratchy and he'd ask for Mama. The letters he'd sent ever since were better than nothing but they weren't really my dad talking.

I'd asked him about him going, when he'd first told Mon and me.

Princess, Monica, I'm going to war. We'll be there a while, but I'll be back. I promise. It was okay that he called me Princess since he didn't do that often. His long face with a pop of red hair had looked very serious and sad, and he was sitting down, hunched over and staring out the window into the sunset.

Monica got up and stood facing away from us some feet, back straight like her lungs were collapsing on her. I knew she was listening. Her ears were practically wrapped around the back of her head.

I took a deep breath. "Why now? Why you?" I'd seen the soldiers in town, wearing their uniforms, and they were all *young*. They didn't have families, or farms, or kids like me.

"Well, honey, it's . . . well." He reached his arm around me like a rope, drawing me to his side. Monica came back over and sat down. His other arm went around her. I sat stock-still. My dad wasn't the hugging kind. "Do you believe in our country?"

"Why sure." How could I not? It was our country, you believed in it.

"Well sometimes, you have to do the thing you believe in most, even if other people think it's crazy. You have to listen to your conscience. And for me," he had said, his blue eyes boring into mine, "this is my duty. Your mama and you girls are going to be fine. I won't be gone for so long." And that was that.

He'd left on a Friday, wearing mottled brown clothes and carrying a bag.

Mama had cried, Mon had cried, but I hadn't. I had to be strong. For him. I'd stood by his elbow as he made his good-byes to the others, and then he'd bent over. He looked so old. There were lines on his face I hadn't seen before.

Take care of the farm and your mama and sister, he'd said, looking at me. *You're in charge. I'm counting on you.*

I'd nodded, and he'd boarded the plane.

And I'd watched the farm ever since.

The lights of my mama's car flashed into my eyes as I sat there in the gathering darkness. She was turning into the drive, which meant it was time for supper.

Ike was something I had to do out of duty, too. Just like my dad and his war. My hand rested on my chest, right above where Ike lay sleeping. I would raise him and keep him alive until he could be safe on his own, far from marauding dogs or wars.

Chapter 10

I met Mama at the garage door. She looked dead on her feet. There were shadows under her eyes.

The door clanged open and she drove inside. I took a deep breath. *Take it easy, P,* I warned myself. *If she doesn't find out now, you've got a chance.*

"Hi, honey," she said, bending out of the car and turning to grab her purse. "Get some of those groceries, would you?" She sounded tired. Then again, she'd been gone since before sunup.

"Sure." I opened the trunk and grabbed a couple of the flimsy plastic bags, eager to turn my back on her. I got through the door of the house and set them carefully on the counter, then ran to my room and got the opened envelope, holding it behind my back. She'd be real excited about that.

"Everything okay with the cows?"

I nodded. "Nothing weird."

"Princess, you weren't down at the river bottoms again, were you?" She frowned at me before she reached down to put the cereal away. Man, it bugged me when she called me by my full name.

"Well, I had to, didn't I? To check the cows?"

She swung around to face me, leaning against the side of the cabinet. "You don't have to go to the bottoms for the cows, Princess. The pasture is up here; the bottoms are pretty far away."

"But—"

"You know what I mean."

I did. She hated me going down to the bottoms when nobody was here.

"I was there, Mama, but only for a while."

"And Blackie?" As she said the dog's name, her eyebrow lifted and I felt like melting and sliding down the sink drain. She knew how much I wanted to be friends with Blackie. Darn it, she'd caught me out.

"Blackie . . . too."

"Princess . . . ," she began, but sighed. "P, you know your dad wouldn't like that." I shrugged a little and looked away to avoid her eyes. They were intense, a minty green that seemed to glow above her green hospital scrubs.

"I know. I'm careful, though." I needed to change the subject before she figured out just what else I'd brought back from the bottoms.

"Joe was here. He killed a snake."

My mama shivered. She had the same dislike of snakes I had, but in her case the dislike kind of extended to the whole farm. She didn't like living out here. She complained about it sometimes, when she and Dad talked.

"He took Blackie, like Dad wanted. And look what I've got." I held out the packet, and her eyes lit up. She looked at me.

"Did you get your letter out already?"

I nodded. She reached out and took the packet, pulling it up close to look at it. She needed glasses but was too stubborn to wear them.

"You read yours already?" She should have known the answer to that question.

"Yeah."

Ike settled down in a different way in my shirt, and I got to wondering if he'd need to go to the bathroom soon. I got all sweaty thinking she could see through my shirt. Could she? She didn't act like it, at least.

The rest of the night passed uneventfully—nobody found out about Ike. Mon sneezed too much for my liking, though, which made me jump every time. I told Mama about Gran calling, and soon enough she and Mon started watching TV, so I made for my room.

The phone rang and I hopped up. Mon's door was shut, with her snoring behind it, and I snuck out of my room to hide behind the kitchen bar that faced the living room.

"Hey, honey." Mama's voice always changed when she talked to Dad. Slower, softer. I hadn't noticed it until lately. I snuck back down the hall and made for her room, picking up the phone slowly, so there wasn't a click. I put it against my ear, being careful not to breathe through my nose.

"—everything's all right with the cows, and Joe killed a snake."

"That's good."

I slumped against the side of the bed. *Dad*. Dark deep voice, with a bit of sharp in it. But there was something wrong with his voice. It sounded old. Or scared.

"You want me to wake up the girls? They'd love to talk to you."

"No." He said it short and low. "They don't need to hear me . . . how I am now." I frowned. What did he mean by that?

I heard Mama make a shushing noise. "They'd love to talk to you."

"Not now, Abigail." There was a pause, and he made a choked sound.

"You're almost home, darling. Only a few more weeks."

I fell asleep thinking about my dad and the cows and how we used to do all the farm work together. He'd always called me his right-hand man, and I'd liked it. There'd been one time we were trying to get the cows in around a storm building up. Blackie was new, I wasn't any good using the stupid donkey to help herd up the cattle, and it had been pretty crazy, what with the wind and rain and lightning.

I dreamed I was walking with my dad and Blackie and we watched as lightning started hitting the cattle, the gunshot crack of it canceling out my hearing as it jumped from animal to animal, the yellow-bright flashes blinding me. I knew my dad would turn it back, like the bull he'd stopped from attacking him when I was younger. He'd just popped it on the nose and it had stopped. In the dream, I stood beside him, confident, watching him. Blackie stood between us, snarling at the lightning strikes. The wind whipped Dad's clothes around, and when the lightning flashed again I saw he was wearing those brown speckled clothes the army makes you wear. His red hair was longer, and his white skin and blue eyes reflected the lightning that crackled all around us. He had a gun, and I wondered why. The storm was coming closer, and the cattle were dropping everywhere I looked as the lightning struck. Their skeletons lit up before they fell.

In one bright flash of lightning, I looked at my dad's face. He was staring at me and frowning. He handed me the gun and I took it, but I looked up to ask him why. When the lightning suddenly jumped over and arced toward him, I yelled like a wild woman and woke myself up.

I looked around frantically, breathing hard.

My door was shut. The sweat from dreaming trickled down my back as I sat up in bed. I wiped tears away as I searched for Ike. There was faint light at the window; it'd soon be time for school.

Where was my possum? He must be hungry. Maybe I'd scared him under the covers with my holler. I looked. Nothing. Had he fallen off the bed? I gasped, fighting back more tears. That was a long way down for a little possum. Leaning over the bed, I called out softly, "Are you there, little buddy? Ike?" I made the little *cheh-cheh* sound he made in desperation. Where was he?

Something stirred beside me, and I turned to face the wall. First a little nose came out, poking pink into the early morning sunlight, followed by eyes, body, and that long, ratlike tail. All my terror fled and I even laughed a little. He'd been sleeping in the pile of pillows I threw against the wall every night.

"Hey, there." I picked him up and he chittered softly, pressing his nose into my hand. "Hungry?"

I was sure tired. I'd fallen asleep with the sight of him resting on a pillow, white fur glimmering in the moonlight. He'd woken me up every couple of hours for food with bright chitterings, little hands on my face—until I woke myself up the last time.

My mama knocked on the door as she headed towards the kitchen. "Up!"

"I already am!" I hollered back.

The bra was lying out, string rolled up beside it. Check. The baggiest clothes I owned, and then . . . my backpack. Check. A soda bottle with some of the milk powder in it, ready to be mixed. Check. A spoon. Check. My jacket. Check. I sighed. I was as ready as I was gonna be. I fought down the butterflies that seemed to have taken up full-time living in my stomach.

After rubbing Ike's little belly to make sure he went real good, I got my own clothes on, bra first. Then I put the possum in. He settled without a sound, long tail sliding up against my side as I picked up my backpack. I checked my side view in the mirror that hung over my dresser, hopping up high enough to see my profile. Nothing but baggy T-shirt. I was good to go.

I opened the door to my mother's face and her raised hand as she prepared to knock again. "Ready?"

"Yeah."

"Okay then."

She straightened her green hospital tunic and smiled at me. Her eyes flicked to my chest and I hurriedly raised my arm up across my side, making sure to cover where my possum slept.

"Princess, are you cold?" She motioned to my jacket and my heart jumped into my mouth.

"A little," I said. I didn't meet her eyes. I didn't know if she'd buy that, seeing as it had been a hundred degrees every day the past month. She pressed her palm against my forehead a moment—cool and clear—and sighed.

"Nothing. Be careful and have a good day. I have to go." She kissed me on my cheek, a waft of perfume filling my nostrils, and she was gone.

As I gulped down breakfast, a horn honked at the front of the house and I ran for it, backpack bumping me—*pound pound pound*—as I flew across the wide lawn. Hopping on the bus, I spotted Mart, his raised hand in the second seat from the front. I sat down on the hard green plastic to a general burst of hilarity from the back of the bus. The high school kids—all the farm kids squished onto one bus—made fun of everybody that moved, outside the bus or in.

"You have him?" Mart was rummaging around in his backpack, and I grinned and nodded.

"Yeah."

"How's he doing?"

"Fine."

He shoved a couple papers at me. I took them, puzzled. "What're these?"

His face was earnest as he took them back from me, pointing out information. "P, come on, you need to scientifically plot the progress of your opossum. Rate of growth, amount of food, all that." His finger teased out one particular piece of paper and he nudged it. "Here is everything an opossum should eat. I made a list for you, see? Milk for a bit longer, then all types of meats—but raw! And vegetables, raw too; and insects, they count."

He went on as I looked at the list. "They can get sick from the wrong kind of food really quickly, so you need to make sure he eats everything on this, and not just meat, potatoes, and lasagna, like you."

I looked at the list. Most of the stuff we had at home, at least when Mama had just shopped. Maybe I ought to sneak some food out before she used it. My eye traveled farther down the list.

"Worms? They can eat worms?" I gagged as we started to

discuss the nasty eating habits of possums. We were still gross-ing ourselves out when the bus driver pulled up to the school, the tin roof over the red bell tower glinting in the sun.

I led the way at a run to the old deserted basketball court. Our school was hardly bigger than nothing. Since we didn't have a lot of kids in the middle and high schools, they'd lumped us all together—four buildings smack dab in the middle of a wheat field. There were lots of little places to hide if you knew them. And boy did I.

We sat down in the bleachers and I fished in my shirt. "Here he is." I brought him out in my hand. Ike wasn't pleased at being woken up. His little mouth opened and he hissed at Mart. "Ike! You don't hiss at friends!" He looked up at me and then back at Mart, mouth gaping open. I was upset, but Mart was smiling and nodding, so I calmed down. Ike hissed a little lower at Mart after another glance at me.

"No, don't get mad at it, P. That's what they're supposed to do." I lowered my hand, not fully convinced.

"You sure?"

"He wouldn't understand it anyway."

I put the little possum back in the sports bra. "Well, what-ever you say. Let's go."

I'm pretty certain it was the longest day of my whole life. I don't know how I got through it. Seemed like every time I got settled down in class, Ike wanted to eat, so I made lame excuses to go to the bathroom. All the teachers gave me funny looks. I had sweaty underarms and it only got worse. We didn't have much for air-conditioning in school and I was wearing my jacket and boy was it *hot.*

Most of the teachers were pretty good about me going to the bathroom—until English. I'd been fidgeting the entire time, and my teacher was a real old badger. She was always one to walk up and down the aisles, and her pantyhose made a *swish swish swish* sound as she stalked sleeping students in her classes. You could always track where she was by that sound. If you were unlucky, she'd catch you with your eyes closed and scare the snot out of you by slamming her ruler down on your desk, just inches from your fingers.

Ike was waking up; he was starting to move around. Mrs. Rock was behind me, just waiting for someone to speak up. I was in one heck of a pickle.

She didn't like me much. She was really old—but not nice old like my gran. Just a mean old woman and that was all there was to it.

But there wasn't any way around it. I'd have to take the chance. I raised my hand and cringed a little. The swishes made their way to my desk and I narrowed my eyes as I looked up. The flourescent lighting flared out around her, turning her gray hair purple through her Coke-bottle glasses, and the wattle of her double chin wiggled threateningly at me.

"What can I do for you, *Miss* Miller?"

"I'd like to go to the bathroom, please." Ike twitched again and I twisted in my seat. She had eyes like one of our setting hens, all beady and staring. I caught Mart watching me from his spot, pencil tapping against his book.

"I don't know about that." I felt my mouth drop open as she continued. "Have you finished your exercises? They're due by the end of class today." I closed my mouth with a snap.

"Well, n-not yet, b-but—" I stuttered.

"But nothing. You can't go until you are two-thirds finished."

"But I need to go to the *bathroom*!" I spit out, and Mart gasped. She didn't look at him but at me as I fidgeted in my chair. Ike was getting more and more awake and was starting to move around in my bra. This was not looking good. "Please!"

She looked around at the other students, who all tried to pretend that their ears weren't glued to our conversation. She couldn't really tell me no, and she knew it. With an irritated sigh, she flapped her hand at me and swished into movement again.

"Fine. Go. But do not dawdle."

Everyone looked back down at their work as I grabbed the milk bottle and spoon with my trembling hand, hiding it under my shirt. Mart smiled at me as I made for the door and I wobbled my lips back at him. I didn't know if I could keep this up a whole week.

I shut the door behind me, walking quickly towards the bathrooms in the old part of the school. The best place for a girl and her possum to hide was back here. When you got to the old part, the floor changed to deep purple carpet and the dark gray walls were shadowy. Just around the corner, and I was there.

"What have we got here?"

Chapter 11

My stomach dropped to my toes as Ike made a very small, very distinct, chirping sound. His nails scrabbled against my skin.

I turned around slowly, smiling nervously at Mr. Sugna, the art teacher. Short, with wiry hair, he spouted French phrases as he told you to correct your painting just *so* before he cried *désolamment,* or take *that* off your sculpture, *chérie! Très bien!*

His squinty little eyes flicked over me, eyebrows bristling like two caterpillars. His red plaid shirt clashed with patched corduroy trousers that sagged over brown leather shoes.

"Just going to the bathroom, sir."

I edged a couple steps towards the bathroom. The milk bottle stuck out from under my shirt, and I stifled a gasp.

"With white milk in a bottle, *chérie*?" His hand gestured towards the bottle and I smiled weakly. What to do now?

"Ah. Well. Um." I stopped in horror as the front of my chest hissed. Barely there, but a hiss nonetheless. Ike stuck his nose out, tenting the shirt across my front, and I just about died.

Mr. Sugna's bushy eyebrows rose up a couple notches, almost meeting the flaky hair above the three ledges of worry lines. His bloodshot eyes bulged as he stared over the top of his glasses at my chest, where Ike's nose moved back and forth. I put an arm up over my chest, but too late.

He took a step back.

I brought my other arm up and crossed them. Ike's nose pressed against my side as my mind raced to find an explanation the teacher would buy. He coughed, and I looked into his eyes. They were dark brown and twinkling.

"Sir?"

"Come *avec moi, Mademoiselle* Preen-cess," he said, and was off, jerking up the steps to the art room. His hunched shoulders slid up before me as I dragged along behind. He didn't wait for me at the top of the stairs, simply unlocked the door and entered soundlessly.

I followed him, cursing my luck all the way. He'd turned the lights on as he'd come in, and I looked around at the room for a moment. Tall shrouded columns of rock sat in the bright sunlight of the late afternoon. Scattered sculpting tools littered the room, and the air was heavy with the scent of cold chalk. Dust motes drifted through the light from the windows and got in my nose as I inhaled.

There was something special about this room. I turned back around to Mr. Sugna and took a deep breath. I had to try to brave this through.

"Sir, I can explain—"

"What have you in your shirt, *chérie*?" He had crossed over to the desks on the other side and sat on one with a fat sigh of relief, his trousers hiking up over his obscenely patterned socks. How could you even buy socks in cat-vomit green with pink triangles?

"I, ah." I hesitated, casting around for anything I could say or do to get him off the subject. Ike was getting worse and worse and moving around something fierce, and I needed to get to the toilet pronto. I pointed at a big rock in desperation. "What a nice stone! What kind is it?"

He was having none of it.

"Come now, Preen-cess. I give you my *mot*. No one will know."

"I have something I'm taking care of! That's all!" I'd have to show him. I pulled out my little possum and poured some milk onto the spoon. Ike churred urgently, little hands reaching out as I brought it within reach. "A possum, Mr. Sugna. I saved him, and now I'm taking care of him."

He moved close to stare at Ike, his eyebrows raised and quivering. I'd never seen hairier eyebrows. Ever. "Oh, I see." He reached out a blunt forefinger, not quite touching Ike as the possum slurped merrily away, and stood back up. "Hmm. *Bien.* You realize that you are not to bring *animaux* to school? *Non non non.*"

"I know it. But look, Mr. Sugna, if I leave him alone right now he's going to die. He's just a little thing and he has to eat every couple hours!" I lifted him up in illustration, causing him to scramble halfway down my arm to reach the milk. Ike *cheh-cheh*'d in panic, liquid dribbling off his whiskers. I brought him back up alongside and he calmed down and continued eating. "I can't do that!"

Mr. Sugna sat back on the edge of the desk, his arms crossed. "*Oui*, I see what you mean." He didn't say anything else as I fed Ike the rest of his food and then did his toilet. When I had slipped him back inside my shirt where he could go back to sleep, the teacher moved off the side of the desk.

"Fine. Then we do this. You come here to feed . . . *le rat.*" His eyes shot to my chest and moved away again. "I'll let it be known you are helping me with a *projet.*"

That was great! I beamed. Before I could get a word in, he continued.

"I'll expect you to come here to feed . . . the *creature.*" He stood up and moved away, his socks bunching up around the bottom of his pants. "This way nothing horrible will happen."

I smiled at him. "Thanks a lot, Mr. Sugna! I'll go back to class now." I got ready to leave, but he was scribbling a note.

"Take this with you. The, ah, *professeur* might have a problem with you being gone so long. Who do you have this hour?"

"Mrs. Rock."

He wrinkled his nose and grinned at me as his eyebrows wiggled genially. "*Oui, certainement* she will have a problem.

Take it." He held it out and I took it, picking the milk bottle back up at the same time. He held a hand out.

"Leave that here. *Maintenant.* You do not need it." I gave him the bottle and spoon and made for the door before he changed his crazy mind.

Come to think of it, he really wasn't all that bad. Pretty normal, actually.

Chapter 12

I hurried as fast as I could, but when I got back to the classroom it was practically time to leave. I only got a chance to sneak up to Mrs. Rock and give her my note before the bell rang. The old battle-ax took it and read it with a look that could have burned paint off walls, but I was scot-free. School was done for the day!

"Remember, class! Friday!" She smirked at me as the other students clustered out, muttering under their breath. I turned to Mart, who'd packed my stuff for me and was waiting by the door.

"What was that about?" I asked him.

Someone reached him before I did. I about fell over when she opened her mouth, instead of ignoring him like she usually did.

"Hello Mar-tin." Cassie Cuter-than-you said, flipping her long blond hair over her shoulder. I wasn't impressed, even when she did her pop-star pout that made her look like a catfish. All gaping mouth and staring eyes. I shouldered past her, grabbing my bag from Mart.

"Thanks, Mart. Let's get out of here."

He cleared his throat, and she shifted to her other foot. What did she want, anyway?

"I'll ah—ah, Cassie? Did you, ah, want something?" He shot me a look I couldn't decipher, and I'd been the recipient of a lot of looks from him. The "save me" looks, the "what now" looks, the "this is gonna hurt" ones right before we both got tanned for something I usually got us into . . . but none of them matched his face right now.

"Mart?" What was wrong with him?

Cassie pushed past me and linked arms. With. My. Best. Friend.

She tugged him around, flipping her hair again so that it lashed my cheek, batting her eyes at Mart. He didn't once take his eyes off her. "We have a prior date, *Princess.*" She said my name in a sour sort of way, and my fists clenched. "Martin doesn't have time right now." With one last glance at me, Mart allowed himself to be steered out of the classroom.

I just stood there, open mouth liable to catch the biggest fly known to man. Like one of those South American ones that could carry off alligators.

When I got on the bus it wasn't much better. Mart sat with her in the same seat, Cassie throwing her hair around like a lunatic and him just taking it. I'd never seen anything like this. I sat across from them, sharing a seat with Jill, a girl from English class. "What in the world is happening there?" I asked her, pointing to where Cassie and Mart sat. Cassie put her hand on Mart's leg and I could see him gulp. Jill stopped giggling and looked at me.

"P, there's a test in Mrs. Rock's class Friday, didn't you know?"

A test. Last day of school. Trust that old bag of an English teacher to stick it to us on the last day of the year. "So . . ."

"So Cassie there wants Mart's help to study for this test—and then she'll just ignore him after. She did it with Billy last time." I think Billy had been Jill's best friend at some point, but he never sat with her anymore.

"So . . ." I still couldn't wrap my head around it.

Jill snorted. "So"—she paused for emphasis, and I looked at her. Her strawberry blond hair whooshed around her face from the wind whipping through the windows, and her eyes were still narrowed on Cassie. If people could shoot sparks out of their eyes, she'd have been blasting. "She'll use him for a good grade in English."

I got up to let Jill out at her stop and sat back down, glancing at them as I did so. His eyes were glassy and he barely responded to her, just mumbled answers. I scooted over to the window and stared out. Knowing why she was doing it didn't help much. My stop came and I practically ran off the bus, hurrying across to the house. I threw my backpack on my bed and flipped around, stomping to the kitchen. Ike jolted along in the bra, asleep.

Shaking my head, I thought about Mart's next few days as I got Ike's food ready.

The perfect crime. He wouldn't know what hit him until the end of the day on Friday. And meanwhile, all she had to do was shake her hair a couple times and make puppy eyes at him to get access to all his notes and his help with her homework. Then she'd act like he never existed.

I'd have to study, but I'd be lying if I didn't say I was something like a whiz in that class. English was my thing. Just spelling wasn't.

I spilled a little milk as I poured it. My hands were shaking.

Did it make me mad, the way she was going to treat him? Oh yeah. But lately Mart was worrying me a little. He was acting funny. Like that whole thing with my chest. I could see his, but he couldn't see mine? They looked exactly the same.

I sighed and shook my head. I wouldn't think about it right now.

I lit out for the pastures and the cows. I'd been inside enough. The cows were all there, but Loosy was still hurt. Maybe worse, even. Green slime trailed down her side, and she bawled. Her calf rushed to her, and I realized it was probably time to think about weaning the babies. I opened the Lookbook.

1. *All cows ok. Loosygoosy still has a cut. Looks like it hurts.*
2. *Do we have to wean?*
3. *Grass yelower.*

I wouldn't call the vet yet. Give it a couple more days, and then he could tell me about the weaning stuff, too.

I had brought out my paper to write Dad, and I carefully drew a picture of Loosy's leg on one of the loose sheets, marking the two scabby cuts with lines and arrows pointing to them. Once I had that done, I walked away from the herd and sat down.

I'd need to be careful there wasn't any hint of Ike in the pages I'd send him.

Dear Dad,

> *We got your letters yesterday. Joe took Blackie just yesterday to work with the cows and I'm sure he's doing good. Loosy has some cuts on her leg, I've drawn them for you. I'll call the vet about them if they don't get better. All the other cows are fine.*

> *I didn't know you could farm camels. That is weird. I wish you were bak, I miss you awful. Maybe you could call one time and I could tell you the farm news that way.*

> *Nothing much else going on. I wish you were here. Mart has been acting weird lately and Callie Smarty-pants tries to act like she's his best friend. It makes me really mad.*

> *Joe shot off his gun again the other day, and killed a goose right above me. It really scared me. Why can't you just tell him to leave it at his house? I don't like it when he brings it. There's no point, and no use for it here.*

> *Love, P*

Chapter 13

By the time it was Friday, I was able to take some big, deep sighs of relief. It looked like the worst of my worries were over. Ike, although wanting to be up for longer amounts of time, managed to stay put and keep me out of trouble at school, which I surely appreciated. It helped that he slept most of the day, even though he was growing like a weed. And Mr. Sugna was great. His idea of me going up to feed Ike in his room worked better than I'd ever expected.

"What do you plan to do with him over the summer, Preen-cess?" He asked as we watched Ike slurp up a spoonful of milk. I considered a little as I poured some more. Ike stuck his tongue out, dancing from foot to foot as he waited.

"Well, Mr. Sugna, I reckon I'll just keep on doing what I'm doing," I said, motioning to the little possum. His tail clenched around my arm, pink against my already brown skin. "I'll get him good enough to be able to stay alive on his own, even though I don't want to let him go."

"Hmm," he said, looking at me a little suspiciously. "So you say. And *chérie*, have you told your mother yet about *le rat*?" He knew calling Ike a rat got a rise out of me. I didn't do anything but shrug and shake my head. "No."

He leaned back on the table and crossed his arms. "And your *papa*?"

I snorted, giving Ike more milk. "Are you kidding? My dad would tan my hide if he ever found out about Ike."

"Really? Why is that?"

"Mr. Sugna, my dad thinks that if an animal is on a farm, it has a job and that's it. There's no such thing as a pet." I stared down at Ike, who was very obviously my pet. "If he found out, I'd be in a whole lot of trouble."

"Then why, *chérie?*"

"Why what? Have Ike?"

Mr. Sugna nodded. "If you know that you will be in *le ca-ca* for it, why do it?"

I shrugged. "I had to. I mean, I had my dad's dog in the bottoms with me, and he killed Ike's mama. I didn't see the sense in letting an innocent little possum die."

Mr. Sugna nodded again and smiled. "I do not see the sense in it either, *ma chère.* So—you have done a good deed, no? There is a little baby alive in the world and he is your *bon ami* because you let your heart decide." At my embarrassed shrug, he bent over a bit to catch my eyes. His eyebrows wiggled up at me.

"I think you have done the right thing. And when it comes time to set him free, because you must, *ma petite,* you will do the right thing. Because you love him."

I couldn't say anything to that. But it made me sound better than I thought maybe I was. It was just what I had to do, that's all.

The possum had finished eating and licked his lips. He bent down and started to lick his feet. I set him down on the desk to give myself some space. The bottle and spoon went back into my backpack, since today was the last day of school and I wouldn't need to be here anymore.

A stench filled my nose and I looked over at Mr. Sugna under my eyelashes. I thought maybe he'd farted on the sly. Nope, the smell was coming from below me. Mr. Sugna sputtered as he whipped his glasses off and cleaned them, jamming them back on his nose to glare at Ike.

"*Le rat* has pooped on my desk!"

Sure enough. I started to laugh as Ike walked a couple steps away and went back to cleaning himself. "Well, he had to go!" I called out to the teacher as he rushed from the room. I giggled and looked around for some towels to wipe the desk. He was able to go by himself! That would sure be an improvement. I loved my little possum, but I didn't like that bathroom thing.

Mr. Sugna came back up and handed me a fistful of napkins. I cleaned off his desk, still chuckling. When I was done, I wiped Ike for good measure and stuck him in my shirt. I stood a little uncertainly at the doorway. It had been real nice of Mr. Sugna to help me out with my little secret this last week. I didn't know how to thank him. He'd turned around and was scribbling something on a piece of paper, which he then gave to me. When I checked it out, it was a phone number. I looked up at him.

"You need any help with your little friend, *chérie*, you give me a call. I'll keep your secret," he said. He smiled and his eyebrows wiggled again. "Have a nice summer."

"Thanks, Mr. Sugna." I smiled back and left before I had to give him a hug or something.

As I slid into an empty seat on the bus, I heaved a sigh of relief. The test was over, the sun was shining, and I had three whole entire months to not worry about school. Now if Dad would just come home and I could keep Ike, life would be perfect.

The bus was one big party, with all the high school kids in the back blaring music. I leaned against the hard plastic seat back, daydreaming. Just me, the big wide open fields, and Ike. A shadow crossed my side vision and a kid slid into the seat right by me. I stiffened a little, like a cow fixing to get a shot in a muscle. Mart looked over at me as Cassie passed by with not a glance our way. When I'd finished glaring at her back, I turned to fully face him.

He looked pretty miserable. The kids who passed our seat looked at him and away, like they were embarrassed or something. Of course I knew Miss Perfect had ignored him immediately after the English test.

Jill had whispered he'd tried to sneak a kiss after school on Thursday. She swore up and down somebody claimed to have seen it, but I couldn't bring myself to believe that. Not Mart. I just looked at him a minute and went back to staring out the window.

"Hi."

"Hi."

Ike stretched, his warm furry body flattening out and thinning in the bra as he scrunched around onto his back.

"How are you? Ike?"

"Fine." I wasn't going to make this easy for him. I was his best friend, after all, and he'd practically ignored me for a week for some girl who probably didn't even know what a possum was.

"Look, I'm-sorry-for-ignoring-you-with-Cassie-I-was-wrong-will-you-forgive-me-please?" He said it all in a rush, his tongue stumbling over the "forgive" and "wrong" parts.

I stared at him a minute, and I know my face looked pretty serious. I glanced out the window, watching the speckles of cows flash past. We hit a pothole, and I jounced a little in my seat. The wind buffeted the side of the bus, and through the open windows you could smell the strong scents of sage and dry grass. The kids in the back of the bus yelled and sang along with the music from the speaker box, soda bottles opening with little hisses and chip bags crackling. I didn't want to fight anymore. The summer was long, and he was an idiot, but a good idiot.

He sat still, watching to see what I would say. I could see him out of the corner of my eye looking straight at me, not fidgeting or anything.

"Okay, you're forgiven. But—" I said, holding up a hand to stop his next sentence, "don't do it again, okay? You should have known better. That Cassie didn't want anything more out of you than studying. You're my best friend, but you really made me mad."

He glanced out the window too and nodded, his eyes fixed on a hawk that wheeled and dipped through the air, matching pace with the bus so that we could see the flash of its eyes as it passed.

"I really *am* sorry," he said.

"I know. Shake on it." I spit into my hand and held it out. He spit into his and shook mine.

I grinned. "So, did you really try to give Cassie a lip-smacker? Did she sprout a tail and horns?"

He rolled his eyes, and we were friends again. I had to laugh.

"What's been going on? How's your dad?"

I frowned and fiddled with my backpack strap. "Well, you know. Still hurt. Nothing else I know of." The nightmares had gotten worse and worse—I couldn't even have the fun first part now without the lightning striking Dad. Most nights I didn't even have to wait for Ike to wake me up. "He's still coming home in a couple weeks," I said. "Mama is getting together a party for him." As the bus pulled up to my stop, I looked over at Mart and felt a little more hope for the summer.

"I'll see you around this weekend?"

He nodded. "Yup."

I could barely keep from kicking up my heels as I got off the bus. Freedom! As soon as I'd changed and fed Ike, I threw all my shoes into the back of the closet. I wouldn't need those until next year!

As I headed off to check on the cattle, I pulled Ike out and looked at him, holding him up so that he could see the farm around us. The sun was shining and Ike was becoming more active. He really seemed to grow by the day. He raised his pink nose and sniffed the air, tail twitching to and fro as I walked.

Blackie bounded and leaped alongside me. I'd brought him, too, just to practice the sitting and being my dog. He'd been in his kennel when I got home. He was actually keeping time with my step, and I was out of school, so I made a song out of it that

I sang full-out as I went along, tromping my way down to the cows.

My little Ike, he's a right good sprite
Sniffing along the tra-il
Twitching along in the Oklahoma light
Happy as a snail!

I couldn't think of any more rhymes, so I just switched the melody around, bellowing it out as I walked. Ike seemed to like it, but he kept scrabbling against my hands, and I thought he might want to sit on my shoulder. Just to test it I put him there, and laughed as he used my hair to pull himself up on top of my head, where he sat, probably looking around for all he was worth.

When I reached the herd, Jezebel's head snapped up and she stared at me, the long grasses she was chewing hanging out of her big mouth. Once she swallowed them she let out a screeching bray and flipped her ears backwards. I could see her stomp her front hoof from where I stood. I hadn't ridden her since the day I found Ike, and obviously she hadn't missed me.

All the more reason to catch her, especially since tomorrow was Saturday. It would be my first day of training Ike for real life.

But if *I* tried to catch *her*, I knew what I'd be up against. Chasing her through sixty acres of long grass was not how I wanted to spend my Friday night. She was as curious as a cat, though.

Glancing around, I saw the cows were all right. Loosy's leg looked to be a little better, even if she still tried to run away from me. I hurriedly updated my Lookbook and pulled Ike off the top of my head.

Time to charm the donkey back to the corral. I took a deep breath and caught her eye. She stood there, neck stretched out like a snapping turtle, just staring at me. As I stood absolutely still, her ears slowly came forward and her front foot went down. Her head cocked to the side. I could tell she was puzzled, and that's just how I liked it. I turned around without another glance at her. Time for my acting skills.

I slumped all down. My head. My shoulders. I melted like ice cream left out in the sun. Even my back got all bent up. I sniffed, and Ike looked up at me quickly and *cheh-cheh*'d. How cute! He must've thought I was sad. I patted his head and waited a minute, took a step, sniffed again.

I smiled as I heard the grass behind me move. She just couldn't handle it, the old donkey. She *had* to know what I was doing. I took another step and sniffed again. Another. Ike kept talking to me, his sweet little *cheh* sounds accompanied by the stealthy sound of a donkey trying to be coy moving through high grass. I laughed to myself and broke into a little sobbing sound like I was bawling, just for some variety.

And like a snake charmer, I charmed my moth-eaten magic carpet down to the corrals.

Chapter 14

I was groggy when Ike woke me up the next morning. My eyes wanted to stay closed and sleep for another hundred hours or so, but nothing doing. The nightmares had come back again last night, and I was beat from chasing Jezebel around yesterday. I'd fought with her the whole evening. She was hard enough to deal with when it was just me, but when I had Ike, she was impossible. She really didn't like him. Once she'd entered the corral, I'd followed her around for hours, Ike in hand. Almost up to the end, she'd snorted and heaved and whistled and run away from me until the corral was one gigantic dust cloud. Eventually, she allowed Ike and me to get close enough to halter her. I knew I had to get on her before I quit for the night or I'd have to turn around and go through the whole rigamarole again on Saturday. In between the nightmares, Ike woke me up a couple of times, too. I'd forgotten to clean out my soda bottle from school, so I'd had to sneak to the kitchen in the middle of the night with a screeching possum to get a cup of warm water. I'd sweated buckets, hurrying as fast as I could through the dark, worrying that he'd wake up Mama and Mon. Taking care of him at night wasn't as much fun as taking care of him during the day. I felt like I was walking through a fog, that's how tired I was.

I rubbed my eyes with my hands and got up. It was time to take him down to the river bottoms. First, I checked Blackie's water and food. "I'll let you out later, boy," I said. He whined as I headed towards the corral. If I thought for one minute that he whined because he wanted to be with me I'd've let him out in a red-hot minute. I knew better.

Time to catch the donkey.

She let me halter her pretty easy, which made me wonder what she was up to. I couldn't hop up on her the normal way, a detail I'd noticed the night before. Usually I used my cracker-jack method, which was handy when you didn't have a saddle. Like me.

"P, you're only gonna ride with a saddle when you can pick up that saddle. I ain't your maid, okay?" My dad always looked so strong and sure, his flannel shirt whipping in the breeze that never fully went away and his hard blue eyes measuring me. He was always measuring me. I know he wanted a boy, but all he got was me.

Since I didn't have any more muscles than a wet noodle and could have never gotten a saddle up on that donkey, I rode bare-back. It was easy enough to get up crackerjack style if you knew what you were doing. You take a couple steps backwards towards her neck, keeping right close to her side, then run forward a couple steps, leaping up with your left foot just as you got past her shoulder.

Normally if I was fast enough I could get halfway up before using my arms to swing a leg over her side. Then *boom*, just like that, I was on. The problem with this method was sometimes I hit my chest when I got up, and I couldn't do that right now or I'd squish the possum. Plus I had my backpack full of food. So I led her up close to the fence. I'd done that when I was first learning to ride, and last night it had worked. I could climb up on the second iron cable bar and hop onto her back from there. It was a good plan, I thought.

But she had a plan too.

Every time I positioned her and climbed up to the second or third cable, she angled her rear away. Not real obvious, and not very much, only a step or two—but too far for my legs to reach over her. On the fourth try, I got down off the fence and we stood eyeball to eyeball. "Jezebel, you're no good. If you don't stand still I'm going to beat you within an inch of your life. Get it?"

She rolled her eyes at me, and I jerked on the halter for good measure.

On the sixth try I made it. Just a couple gates to navigate out of the honeycomb of corrals. We got through the last gate and headed onto the road and the bottoms, me rocking gently on her bony back as she walked along, ears forward. Her cloppy hooves sounded hollow on the rock road. I took Ike out of my shirt and plopped him on my head, where he hung on with his little hands and feet.

There's nothing prettier than Oklahoma grassland in the summer. Waves and waves of long grass, some already golden from the harsh sun and no rain, swayed gently along the sides of the road as far as the eye could see. Well, it wasn't a road in a *real* sense, with pavement and everything. It was more a flat-topped stretch with rocks from the railroad dumped on top of it. They did it every year, the railroaders—the city would fill big dump trucks with rocks from the old railroad lines and dump them on rutted country roads. Then a few days later, a big bulldozer would slam its way through, pushing and tamping the rocks down. The worst thing was all the railroad spikes mixed in with the rock. They were long and sharp and could slit a car tire like a knife.

I took a deep sniff. Oh, the smells! They were as distinct as the beautiful grasses and stunted trees that dotted the landscape. The slight scent of alfalfa, its pretty purple heads bobbing in the field across the way. Almost too sweet when it mixed with the sage that littered the side of the road like so many weeds. When you took a deep whiff and got a nose full of the ragweed pollen that was always on the wind in summer, you'd cough until the hot, rich smell of honeysuckle chased all that nasty out and made your mouth water instead.

I could almost tell where we were along that road just from the smells. The little creek by us, wheat out by Buckham's place, then the alfalfa field, Cassie Knight's dad's cattle field, the river crossing, and we were there. . . . I shut my eyes, just to prove to myself I could do it.

Jezebel's hooves took on a high echoing sound and at the same time I smelled a damp, dark smell. We were far enough away from the house to be by the tiny creek, then. It had lots of crawdads and little baby fish in it, though it wasn't deep enough for bigger fish.

I stopped for a moment at the edge of the first bridge, looking down. The water was bronze brown, with little shivers of silver that slipped through the ripples. I knew if I stepped into the creek I'd sink up to my knees in the squishy mud the crawdads skimmed over. I had work to do, though. I'd save it for another day. I kicked Jezebel forward and she moved into the slow bouncy walk she favored, me drumming my heels along her sides. Whenever she had to take me anywhere she did her darndest to take choppy steps, especially if I made her walk fast. She was real uncomfortable to ride when she did it, too.

We were almost there. We'd already passed Cassie's dad's place and were crossing the big bridge. Jezebel didn't like the way her hooves sounded on the bridge, so she always went over it a little faster, hoof echoes shimmering off the high canyon walls as she hurried across. Her unshod feet made a *chuk chuk* sound as she reached the rocky road again. I took a good look around as we came up to the farm entrance, and tucked Ike back down in my shirt. It really wasn't an "allowed" exploring area, but I'd never actually seen anybody there. Still, it never hurt to make good and sure it was empty before going in. We stopped by the broken-down mailbox, and I looked around to make sure we were safe. Nope, nobody.

I thumped Jezebel into a trot. She went forward with ramrod-straight legs to get me back, making me bob up and down on her back like a pogo stick. I neck-reined the silly thing into the dirt drive, riding past the deserted house with no more than a glance.

We came up to the gate, and I got ready to grab the small rope that held it closed. Jezebel kept angling her butt away from the gate, so I really had to reach out.

"Excuse me?"

Chapter 15

Jezebel snorted and hee-hawed, jackknifing around to face whoever'd spoken. My hands were flying around everywhere—holding the donkey, holding Ike, trying for balance, grabbing scruffy mane.

As I fought to stay on I kept catching glimpses of the visitor. A dirty white Stetson cowboy hat. A muffled red-and-black-plaid shirt. A black truck parked behind him, not visible from the road.

Crap. I was in trouble.

I finally got Jezebel under control and turned to face him fully. He was tall and wide, and stood in the sunlight, shadow blacking out his face. "Hello, sir."

In all my summer, winter, fall, and spring days of sneaking onto this patch of land, I'd never ever seen him. The man moved closer, studying me from underneath his hat. I got ready to run if I had to. He saw me picking up the lead rope and his body relaxed. He pushed back his cowboy hat and came closer. I held the reins tighter.

"It's awright, girl, don't worry. What you doin' down here?"

His voice was gravelly but seemed normal, and I relaxed a little. When he moved out of the sunlight to where I could see him, I blinked. He was really old—like fifty or something. His hair was all white where I could see it under his hat, and his eyes were ice blue. They stared up into mine as I thought around for an answer. When I didn't respond right away, his forehead crinkled as he thought.

I looked down at myself and thought I probably looked like an idiot sitting there on top of my donkey, with my hand against my chest and dirty feet dangling down her sides. Apologizing seemed a good way of figuring out who this guy was without asking.

"Sorry, sir, but you have the nicest land I've ever been on. I live back there a-ways." I flapped my hand towards my house, but not exact, just in case. "I come down here to, ah . . ." I let it trail off and looked at him closely.

"You *did* come down here for a reason, darlin'?" He shifted legs, one hip coming back underneath him with the other jutting out. His knee popped and I jumped, blurting out everything at once.

"I have to teach my possum about life and your place is just perfect, I'm sorry I don't know who you are—"

His eyebrows raised up and his face cracked into a smile. "Seriously? A possum? You got a possum there?"

I nodded and slid off Jezebel's back, landing with a soft thud in the dirt. It puffed up around my bare feet as I pulled Ike out of his hiding place. I stepped up closer to the old man and held out Ike, who looked up into the old cowboy's eyes. Ike squinted, at him, then hissed, white mouth shining. The man leaned back and away from the possum, eyes focused on him.

"See?"

"Yes indeedy, I surely do." His gnarled finger reached out and gently touched the tip of Ike's nose. The little possum sniffed it and sneezed, turning it into a hiss halfway through. We both laughed.

The man's eyes were real pale, with dark rings around them, and lots of wrinkles around the edges that looked like he must smile a lot.

"I'm sorry, Mr. . . ." He came to and whipped his cowboy hat off. "Sorry, little lady, name's Knight, Jesse Knight," he said, with a short little nod of his head. He reached a hand over and I shook it.

"Cassie's dad?" This man surely would have nothing to do with Cassie. He was so nice!

He was nodding and smiling. "Well, you know my little Cassie? She's my granddaughter."

"School." I mumbled, saddened. How could this guy be related to that piece of work?

He grinned again. "Well, that's nice. I'll tell her I saw y—"

"No no," I said, backing away hastily. "No need to do that. She doesn't . . . I mean, um, nobody knows . . ." I lifted my hand and he seemed to get it. His eyebrow quirked up.

"You mean to say nobody knows about your little friend there?" He smiled again. "Then don't worry; your secret is safe with me." He looked down at Ike and his expression softened. "I had a little possum like that once, long time ago. Best friend I ever had." He looked at me real steady, and I tried to stand up straighter.

"Well, girl, be my guest, then. It's my land, and I'll give you the okay here and now. Use the corral back behind there for your jenny. Just let her loose there, she won't cause no trouble."

I must have looked at him amazed, because he just chuckled and reached over to open the gate with a tug. "I've wondered where those tracks were coming from for a while now. Go on. You'll be fine in there. Keep an eye on the fences, hey? Let me know if there's anything wrong out there. Perfect place that it is." He laughed again as I started forward.

"Oh, and girl?" I turned to him, Ike on my shoulder.

"One more thing."

"Yes, sir?"

"You be careful down there, hear? I've had to shoot a couple raccoons with the rabies."

I nodded. "I've heard about it, sir. I'm being real careful. And thanks—a lot!" I slid through, pulling Jezebel behind me, and smiled at him. He smiled back and shut the gate.

Wow. So not all of that family were horrors. To hear my dad talk, you'd think they were all fire-breathing four-headed monsters. But Jesse Knight was okay. Better than okay, in fact.

I stuck Ike in my shirt when I got to the little corral and opened the small gate, waving Jezebel through. She snorted at me and ducked out of her halter, going over to the full trough of hay. There was water too. She'd be busy there and happy.

I pulled Ike out and brought him up to my nose. Black eyes stared into mine and he panted slightly from the heat. I shouldered my backpack better, and smiled at him. "Time for your school, little buddy." We turned and set off for the canyon.

Chapter 16

I don't think there was anybody as happy as me in the whole world as I set off down into the canyon. The sun was shining, it was a Saturday in summer, and I had a backpack stuffed with sandwiches and water, alongside a nice bottle of milk for Ike. We could stay out here the whole day. Which was probably what we'd do.

The old worn cattle trail wound its way down through the red-dirt hills lined with cobbled-together cheatgrass and prairie wildflowers. If you just stared from the top of the hill, you wouldn't see any of the beauty that was the bottoms. You had to look underneath the surface. Once you did, it was like entering heaven. The wind became cool and welcoming, bringing smells of white-hot hay and flowers and dancing with whiffs of cottonwood fluff. You could hear the meadowlarks singing *tir-tir-tirtirtir,* which rose sweetly over the rather hesitant bob-white calls of the quail that hid in the tall yellow grass. I stopped for a moment and stood, my eyes closed. The cottonwood leaves crackled, adding *rat-a-tat-a-tat* sounds to the mix. I opened my eyes and continued on down. Once my bare feet touched the damp ground at the bottom, I turned and weaved through the vine-covered trees to my little camp. It was pretty far from where I'd found Ike, but this was enough like his territory that he could learn everything he needed.

I slung my backpack onto a tree branch and surveyed my little campsite fondly. It was located under an old crabapple tree, the branches gnarled and twisted high above my head. The ground was tamped hard underneath. I put Ike down and he nosed around as I checked my supplies. I had some things hidden here in the branches where I knew varmints wouldn't get them: rope, some matches, and a couple bottles of soda.

Not even ten steps away, the creek gurgled as it passed a particularly deep spot. I'd managed to drag a big rock over to the edge, and often used it to sit on and dangle my feet in the water, the minnows nibbling my toes as I read. The heat of the cruelest Oklahoma day couldn't reach me down here.

I looked up to the right. In the only bright patch of sunlight around the tree, a very shallow section of creek with a good sand base stood still and waiting. It was perfect for our first water lessons. Later, after the lesson, there was a particular wild peach tree farther down the creek that would provide our dessert.

Since I didn't know when Ike should be weaned, and I'd memorized that printout of Mart's that described what a normal possum would eat, I'd decided to start teaching him now. Even if he wasn't hungry he'd remember it when the time came. I pulled him up to eye level. "Ready, buddy?" I set him down onto the ground again after a quick look around. I made my sneezing sound. He *cheh-cheh*'d and took a step towards me. He practiced walking and climbing in my room at night. I'd wake up sometimes from a tug on the bedclothes as he pulled himself up the side. He was always happy to curl up in bed, though; even the carpet wasn't as nice and comfy as all the pillows jammed over to the side of my mattress. He was bigger, too, I noticed, doubling in size nearly every time I looked at him.

I took a step forward and to the right, towards the water, and he followed me slowly. Then another step. Ike seemed to float from side to side like a duck in deep water, and his nose was everywhere as he came along, eyes on me. Something caught the light behind him. I glanced and froze. There, in the shadows, was a raccoon. I swooped down and grabbed Ike quick as a lightning strike, yelling out to scare the raccoon away. I grabbed a stout stick and crouched down, the stick raised, ready to defend myself.

Raccoons almost *never* come out in the daylight. Those that do could have rabies. This one didn't move, and I just crouched and listened to the thunder of my heart in my ears. Finally I stood up and carefully eased my way forward to the raccoon. My stick was raised, ready to defend if necessary. When I got close enough I saw it was dead. It hadn't been for very long. And I could see why. I examined its bared teeth with a shudder. Dried bits of foam still flecked the sides of its mouth. Its eyes—what I'd seen glittering—were crinkled up like it was in an absolute fury.

I shivered and stood up. It couldn't stay like this; if some other animal ate it, that animal could get rabies, too. I whipped the Lookbook out and wrote:

Racoon found. Dead. Can other animals get sik from him?

Twitching, I dug a hole as deep as I dared, as close as I could get. Ike had wanted to sit on my shoulder, but my digging was too energetic for him, so instead he'd clambered up on top of my head and watched all the doings from there. When I was done with the hole, I used the stick to push the raccoon in. It landed with a thud, and I shoved the dirt over it quickly. Once it was covered, I used the same stick to break up the dirt it'd been lying on, stirring it around. With a sharp heave, I pushed the tip of the stick that had been touching the raccoon as deep as possible into the ground, and took a deep breath, shaking.

Then I turned and ran for the water, a hand on top of my head to steady Ike. We reached the river and I bent down, scrubbing my hands for all I was worth. I sat down on the sand and stared at them as I thought. It had been rabid. I was almost certain of it. It was a close call. I shivered, thinking what my dad would say if he knew I could have been attacked by a rabid 'coon just for an ol' baby possum.

Should I go home? Everything in me said no. I'd done good, I thought. I could run fast. Going home wouldn't get Ike any closer to knowing what an adult possum ought to know. No, I'd stay. I straightened my shoulders and set Ike down beside me on the rock. The water was real clear, and thin strands of kelp floated in it, lodged on half-submerged twigs. Minnows dashed around, adding their quicksilver glints to the sparkles on the surface of the water. I looked for something for Ike to eat.

He watched me closely as I stuck my hand into the water and wiggled it around, showing him how the water rippled. It felt good. I pulled out a tiny snail that jammed back furiously into its shell as I turned and held it out to Ike. Was he hungry enough to eat it? Did he even know what it was? He reached up and sniffed and I set it down in front of him. He didn't sit up on his haunches as he did when he slurped his milk. Rather, he pushed the snail along in front of him, inquisitively, and licked his nose where it had made contact with the shell. He moved forward, his little pink fingers reaching out to grasp the snail and turn it over. He snuffled around the opening where the little animal lived and looked up at me, for all the world like, "Well, now what do I do with it?"

I smiled and waited.

The snail had edged out of the opening and was casting around for a way to get righted again. I guess it thought it had fallen over. Ike looked back down and I could've sworn that his eyes got all sharp and aware. He reached down, quick as a shot, and bit the top of the snail, pulling the soft body out with a tug. He chewed a little, looking at me.

"Well, look at you! Good boy!" Amazing how quickly an obviously brilliant possum could learn.

"That's the way, Ike! We'll get you every kind of food, so you won't be picky and you'll know what to look for when you want something to eat!" He *cheh-cheh*'d a couple times at me.

I'd been confused about that for a while before Mart had set me straight. "It's how they call their mamas, P," he'd said. "It just means that he thinks you're his mom, and that's how he calls out to you." It gave me a warm feeling, just thinking about it. He could depend on me, and I'd never let him down. Ever since the second day or so, he'd used it when it felt like he wanted my approval, or like he was asking and answering a question.

He finished the snail and dropped the shell on the ground, then walked a few steps and sniffed at the water. Even tested it a couple times with his long, delicate pink tongue. Evidently deciding that the water wasn't as good as milk, he sat down on his back legs, hoisting his front into the air. I watched, fascinated, as he started to clean himself, licking fastidiously between his toes. Was it something he'd taught himself to do? Or remembered from his mama? Instinct, maybe? I'd never cleaned him like that. His feet rubbed across his ears as good as any cat I'd ever watched, his little fists all bunched up as he dragged them across his hair. He only did it a couple times, and then he dropped back onto his forelegs and *cheh-cheh*'d at me sleepily. I laughed.

"Come on." I reached down and picked him up. "Let's go see if those peaches are ripe."

They were, and better than any I'd eaten from a store. I crammed peach after peach in my mouth, spitting the pits into the creek to be washed downstream. I had Ike lick the sweet-tangy goodness off my fingers before I washed them in the clear creek water. Heaven.

I heard a honking sound like the kind of horn you'd have on a bicycle, and I turned to see my bud Mart coming down the hill on his four-wheeler. His face was pale and set. "Good thing I found you, P. You gotta come with me."

"Mart, you aren't supposed to be down here with the four-wheeler."

He shook his head. "You need to come with me right now. No time."

The sharp diesel scent canceled out the pure sweetness of the peaches. "What's up?"

Mart looked anywhere but at me and took a deep breath. "You need to get home quick," he said, and motioned back towards my house. "Something's happened to your dad."

Chapter 17

My jaw dropped and I squeezed Ike so hard he squeaked. "Happened? What do you mean, something's happened?"

"I don't know."

I jerked forward and scuffled over to him right quick, jumping on the back of the four-wheeler.

"Your mom just called me, said to find you—"

"Just go!" I cried out, stuffing Ike back inside my shirt as the four-wheeler roared to life. He turned around and headed back the way he'd come, back towards the gated entrance.

All the hairs on my skin seemed to be trying to leave it. Happened to Dad? What more could have happened? He was stuck far away, hurt, and something else had happened? When we got to the gate I tugged on Mart's arm, motioning him to stop. I couldn't leave Jezebel here. Mart looked at me with worried eyes. I think I was crying. "Go on ahead, I'll get Jezebel and follow you." He nodded and drove off, for once going above the minus two miles an hour he usually did.

I blasted through the corral and grabbed Jezebel. She must have known I meant business, because for once in her fool life she didn't fight me or anything, just stood still until I'd gotten up. The world around me seemed to blur as she galloped for home.

There were cars parked all over the driveway of my house. It looked like the barn raising my dad had some years ago, when people from all over came for a day to help build our big white barn.

Dad.

I pulled Jezebel to a halt in front of Mart, but it took a couple seconds to figure out why he was standing there with his hand out. "You go on inside," he said. "I'll take care of Jezebel." She snorted and backed away a little. I just slid off and tossed him the reins.

"Okay. Thanks." I took a deep breath and straightened my shoulders, heading for the door. My possum was still in the bra as I walked inside. It looked like our four closest neighbor families had come over.

"Princess!" Mama was sitting on the couch, with my sister crammed up right beside her. They both had red-rimmed eyes. Mama *never* came home from work early.

Shock on shock pounded on me, and I felt like a piece of cottonwood fluff in the wind, being swirled this way and that. I stood in front of her and opened my mouth, but nothing came out. *Dad.* I pushed past the fog in my head and tried again. "What happened?" My voice cracked. I flushed and coughed to clear my throat, trying not to sound so little and sissy. Like a *girl.*

Mama dabbed at her eyes with a napkin.

Mon sniffed loudly, and in the corner, Mr. Laloun from down the road was talking urgently into the phone, making notes on a piece of paper. The other people stood like sentries in the living room and what I could see of the dining room, talking low-voiced, with eyes cast down. One held a broom, while another had a casserole in their hands.

Mama sighed. I rubbed my damp hands on my T-shirt. "A call came today. The hospital where your dad was recuperating was attacked, and they're bringing everyone back to Walter Reed Hospital in Maryland. They told me he was in critical condition, but details were pretty foggy."

"Critical?"

Mama looked determined. "Critical. They didn't say I could come, but I didn't ask, either. I'm going, as soon as Mr. Laloun can get the ticket." Mr. Laloun straightened his shoulders and looked our way.

Mon ducked her head, so I couldn't see her eyes. Her other hand was clutching Mama's; I saw the whiteness of her knuckles as she gripped it. Mama moved a little in her seat and Mon spoke up, her voice all hollow sounding. "I'm going too, for you, Mama." Mama squeezed her hand and I was separated and alone.

"That's fine, Mon," Mama said. She turned to me, her green eyes staring intently into my blue, scared ones. "Do you want to come, honey?" I stood there, frozen.

I wanted to; I wanted to, *bad.* So much I ached for it. But: *Take care of the farm,* Dad had said. *I'm counting on you.*

I sighed and shook my head. "Mama, I can't go. I promised Dad. I *promised* him."

Mon jumped on me like a rabid coon, her runny red eyes glaring at me before Mama could say anything. "You stupid hick, you want to watch this stupid farm and not be with your dad?"

My jaw dropped. "Why do you care all of a sudden? You told me he wasn't even your dad!" I shook with the urge to pop her.

"I didn't mean it, you know I didn't mean it," she said softly. I shut my eyes, fighting to hold back the tears.

"Girls. Honey, are you sure?" Mama reached her hand out to me and after a moment I took it. It was freezing cold.

"I promised him, Mama."

She closed her eyes and squeezed my hand. "Okay. We've got to find somebody to watch you while we're gone."

I shrank back. "I can take care of myself."

"No," she said, looking around at the people. "You can't."

I couldn't take care of myself? The dead coon flashed in front of my eyes as a burning fire started in the pit of my stomach. It spread from my stomach to my chest and to my neck—I was afraid when it got to my mouth I was going to say something I would feel really bad about.

I didn't have a chance. There was a commotion at the door. For the second time that day, my jaw dropped clear down to my stomach, and my anger disappeared.

Mart's mother was making her way through the crush of people, and Mart dragged along behind her, a runty calf being jerked behind a massive roping horse. "Darling!" Mart's mom had a low but very loud voice that cleared out other conversations and somehow snagged everyone's attention. She was very tall, very blond, and very solid. "How *are* you doing?"

"Petunia." Mama nodded. I hadn't known her name was Petunia. Mama raised an eyebrow at me. I didn't want to miss anything, but she wanted a seat for the woman.

I grabbed a chair from the dining room, dragging it over for Mart's mom to sit in, and slid a glance at Mart.

"Sorry," he whispered as he sidled up to me. "She must have heard me on the phone when your mom called looking for you and was ready like a shot." I nodded.

Her voice rose above the din again. "Of *course* we can watch over your dear, ah, Princess." I stared at Mart in shock, and I was talking before I knew it.

"No way, Mama." All eyes turned to me. "If anybody, Gran. Gran or nobody. It's my way or the highway." Gran could do it. She was planning to visit anyway.

Mama held her hand out and I took it again. It was a little warmer.

"Okay, honey, if that's what you want. I'll call Gran and ask her. Thank you so much for the offer, anyway, Petunia," she said. "It was very neighborly of you to volunteer."

Petunia smiled back and I felt bad. I had nothing against her, but more against the whole situation. After a moment, she made her excuses and left. Mart threw me a look and a shrug before he followed her.

Mama was staring off into space, so I followed them out.

Mart was on his four-wheeler over by the swing set, and I went to sit on a swing next to him. The blue sky was dark and the chain links felt hard and cold under my hand. I stared down and took a deep breath. "Mart, you know why I can't go, right? The farm. I promised Dad. I know Joe will come by to check on things, but I promised."

Mart nodded. "I know, P," he said.

Chapter 18

After Mart and the neighbors left, I tromped back inside. The house was dark and silent, even though it was still light outside. The air-conditioning was colder than it'd been since I could remember, and I shivered.

I snuck into my room and fed Ike quick, and then stuck him in my shirt and went back to my parents' room. Mon was there, curled up like a rattler in the side chair. Mama was packing.

They looked up as I entered. Mama took a deep breath. "I'm leaving tonight, honey. Fred is taking me to the airport in an hour." I stared at her, dismayed. Already?

"Just you? Isn't Mon going?"

She shook her head as she grabbed some button-up shirts from Dad's supply. "No. I'll call you once I'm there. Gran will be here tomorrow morning. She was happy you'd thought of her." There was a warm stab in my heart.

Mon sneezed and I edged away from her, back towards the door. "I thought you said you were going!"

Mon looked at me with thunder in her eyes.

"No, she's staying."

"Why?" Mon *finally* wanted to see Dad. Then they told her no?

Mama sighed. "Honey, Gran is so *old*—ah . . . er. She may need Mon's help around here. And to be here for you."

Mon snorted. I knew she wouldn't throw water on me if I was on fire, especially now.

"We'll be okay if she goes, really. I can help Gran."

Mama looked over at Mon. "I know you want to go with me and I appreciate it, honey, but I'll be all right. I can handle things there."

Mon jumped to her feet, staring at both of us. Her hair was out of its clasp and it straggled down against her cheek. "I don't agree with this, do you hear? Just because the hick needs a baby-sitter, I have to let you deal with this alone! It's not right!" She sneezed violently again. "I'm obviously allergic to her!"

She ran out of the room and slammed her bedroom door.

I sat and watched in silence as Mama finished packing.

A little over an hour later, Mon and I watched Mr. Laloun's car ease out of the driveway, Mama waving from the window. I raised a hand, kind of; Mon choked back a sob, turned around, and went inside the house. I petted the front of my shirt where Ike lay, then walked around the side of the house near the trees my dad had planted. I pulled the possum out and set him down—and was kind of astonished. He was getting big; his body was longer than my hand, and his tail seemed to be growing, too. He was also getting more and more interested in his surroundings, and he slept less. He snuffled around as I frowned. How would I keep him a secret from my gran? She was great, don't get me wrong. But she had eyes like a hawk, that was no lie.

The front door slammed and I grabbed Ike and stuffed him into my shirt. I turned around to see my sister come around the front. I crossed my arms over my chest and waited for her. She sneezed a couple of times as she walked across the lawn. She'd probably have an allergy attack and I'd catch heck because she had to come outside to talk to me.

"Go away," I said. I started to leave, but she grabbed my arm and I jerked to a stop. Ike changed position in my shirt a little, but not enough for her to notice. "Just say what you're going to say and get lost."

"I'm sorry."

My mouth dropped. She sneezed again, and then sucked on her inhaler.

"Beg pardon?"

"Look, I'm sorry. I'm really sorry about everything." She paused and looked down at her pink toenails. "I didn't mean to get mad at you, or be mean about Dad." Her toe dug into the grass.

"Let's go inside. It's not healthy out here for you." I could be nice too.

We walked slowly back to the door together, and I realized I was talking to my sister without fighting for the first time in months.

She slumped down on a bar stool. "I didn't mean it. I didn't mean it!" she said, almost crying. "I was just mad he didn't want to talk to me! I didn't mean to say he wasn't my dad!" I stared at her. She sniffed, and sneezed, and sniffed again. "I . . . want to tell him I'm sorry."

"When you talk to him next."

"Yeah."

Then I had a great idea. "Why don't you write him a letter and tell him? I'll write him too, and we'll send them to this Walter Reed place." I bet Mart could get me the address from the Internet.

She looked up, smiling a little. "That's a good idea, P."

I smiled back.

That night I had the worst nightmare yet.

Chapter 19

While I waited for Gran the next morning, I worked with Blackie for a while. I'd tried and tried to get him to sit for me. He still wasn't having anything to do with it—although he did lick my hand after I bribed him with a chunk of cheese.

In fact, it was almost one P.M. when Gran rolled in, her old pink Cadillac's hood catching the sun just right and blinding me as she turned into the driveway. I ran alongside, smiling, waving both arms. I knew Gran would want to hug me, and a little possum squished up against my chest would not be a good thing, so Ike was having his very first alone time in the room. I didn't think he'd mind too much. He was investigating a book, his nose shoved deep in the page crevice as I'd shut the door.

"Gran!"

"Fishstick!" I smiled broadly and leaped up to hug her lean body. She swatted at me with her long hands and rested them gently on the top of my head. "Fishstick, you're getting huge! I almost didn't recognize you!" I pulled back to look at her, laughing.

She never changed. She was about 800 years old or something, her wrinkled skin hanging off her in draping curtains, but you didn't see all that once you got to talking to her. Her eyes sparkled blue and snappy, and her Texas accent washed over me like a welcome rain after a long drought. She never wore jeans, and I'd never seen her in slacks, either. She was strictly a skirt kind of girl.

I leaned in for another hug, trying not to laugh but feeling so happy there seemed to be something stuck in my throat.

She had blue hair this time. She always got her hair dressed at the beauty college. My mama called it the school for the clinically untalented. I couldn't remember all the different hairstyles she'd had—or the colors. Right now it was eggshell blue with tight curly hairs like you'd see on a sheep. Not as bad as the bright red verging on pink, or the black-with-a-white-streak mohawk thing. But pretty bad still.

"How you doing?" She pulled me to her once, hard, and looked up. "Where's Monica?"

I shrugged and looked at her from the corner of my eye. "Aw, Gran, you know Mon. She's inside having issues and sneezing."

Her short bark of a laugh made me giggle, and she turned to shut the door. "Issues and sneezing, huh? Well, help an old woman in and get her bag, would ya?"

"Gran, you wouldn't be old even if you were a hundred and thirty-two." But I still ran to open the back car door. There sat her cornflower blue leather suitcase—and perched on it, one thick chocolate bar. I don't know how she did it, keeping the chocolate on top of that suitcase—unless she drove like Mart did, of course.

"All this in here for you?" I asked with a grin.

"Bring it inside, you rascal. I've got to visit the ladies' room." She disappeared into the garage, her lean body moving storklike as she bent her head under the door. She said she didn't know where Mama had come from, she was so short. I was impressed to see I was finally getting to be as tall as her.

I inhaled the chocolate as I lugged that old suitcase into the house. I didn't know how some dresses could be so heavy, but they sure were.

I could hear her singing as I got inside. She had a real true voice, high and sharp, and she sang almost all the time, like a robin. She used to sing with her four sisters during the Great Depression.

I heaved the suitcase into Mama and Dad's room, and then ran to my room to check on Ike. I nearly crushed him as I opened the door. "What's wrong, little buddy?" He ran across my feet, chirring at me. I picked him up, smoothing his fur, which was as ruffled as the feathers on a setting hen. He snuffled at my hands. Had he been scared?

"Fishstick! You in there?" Gran was at the door and banging, and I stuck Ike in my shirt quick. He settled right down, and I guess that was what he'd wanted. To be close to me.

"Yeah! Give me a minute!"

Chapter 20

I sat and chatted with Gran as she whipped together a nice big meal from the fixings Mama had left.

"You get a letter from your dad recently, P?"

"Yeah, he wrote about four days ago." I shrugged. "Just about farm stuff, though."

"Soon you'll see him in person."

I didn't know how I felt about seeing Dad after all this time, so I just sniffed.

Gran cooked every time she was up to visit—her famous Texas chicken, fried in hot oil; garlic mashed potatoes with smooth brown gravy; corn on the cob; and biscuits. My mama cooked good, but my gran could fix a meal for the devil and he'd sell *his* soul to *her* for the recipes.

The good smells must have lured Mon in. She sidled up and sat on one of the other bar stools and joined the conversation. It had been a long time since Monica had been around me so much.

Gran slapped everything on the kitchen table, pulled her apron off, and we all dug in. When you bit into that chicken, you'd first get the crispy taste of the batter. . . . She used corn-meal and all sorts of herbs mixed up, her secret recipe. Then you'd sink past the batter and down into the chicken. That Colonel guy had nothing on her.

My favorite way of eating it was to take a bite of chicken, about the biggest bite I could, some mashed potatoes, a bit of corn, and then shove it all farther in with biscuit until my cheeks pouched out like a squirrel's. I could go almost a whole morning and afternoon on one of Gran's meals. Her food really filled you up.

There wasn't much conversation as we ate; prissy girl or no, Mon was real fond of her food, too. As we finally sat back in our seats (thank goodness I was wearing elastic shorts!), Gran sighed and took a deep drink of water. "What's on your schedules today, girls?"

I spoke up first. "Dad told me in his letter to weed the garden." She looked at me approvingly. "Oh?"

I sat back farther, bracing against the chair's back. "Yup. He said Mama didn't have time to do it." It was an outside chore, so technically mine anyways.

She smiled at me and glanced at Mon. "You, Monica?"

"Nothing much. I'll clean up, since you cooked, and maybe go into town later with Julie."

Suddenly Ike lifted his head and I looked down in horror as my T-shirt tented out. Time I was going. I coughed and spoke up. "Well, I'll be outside then." Ike twisted in my shirt, and Gran nodded. Taking that as her permission, I hopped up from the table and lit off for my room.

Ike was chittering and hungry as I lifted him out of the bra, and I quickly poured him a bowl of milk. He lapped it up. He'd graduated from the little spoon as soon as he was able to go to the bathroom on his own, and he seemed to like being able to stick his whole nose under the surface and slurp. I had to be sure to get him outside real quick after he ate, though; it seemed to go right through him. I changed while I waited for him to finish. Once he was done, we headed outside. First, I'd let Blackie out a bit. He whined and came up to the gate as I approached.

"Hey, Blackie. Sit." My jaw dropped as he sat right in front of me. *He sat!* I couldn't believe it. He got back up and his stub tail wiggled all over as he stared at me. When I opened the gate, he bounded through, and with a lick for my knuckles, raced past me. A lick and a sit—this was my lucky day!

I had to try it now that he was out. "Sit." He sat. I laughed. Holy cow! The dog was listening to me!

"Good boy!" I slipped him a cheese chunk I'd snuck from the kitchen and headed over to the garden. "Let's go."

We went, Blackie flopping down under the eave of the roof, panting up a storm. I couldn't believe he'd listened to me three times in one day.

I surveyed the garden spread out before me. Scads of vegetables were already there, and while I didn't eat many of them, Gran and Mon would. I'd need to pick the ripest to take in. The garden was twice the length of our house, filled with corn, potatoes, and leafy things like zucchini, tomatoes, and lettuce. Even if they weren't fully ripe right now, they were good enough for my little possum.

I went to the garden shed and took out a hoe and a rake. I'd start on the early ripe cherry tomatoes; they were my gran's favorite food. Bring enough of those sassy red things inside and she'd never look anywhere but at them.

Ike squirmed in my shirt. I reached in and pulled him out. "Hey, little buddy. You want to be out?" He chirred at me and I grinned. I set him carefully at the edge of the garden. He waddled along behind me, bright eyes observing everything.

A black shadow swooped in from my right, and I grabbed Ike just as the dog reached us.

Chapter 21

It was almost like having a dog of my own, and I liked it. Blackie danced and wiggled around, sniffing the ground where my little possum had stood a moment before. I couldn't tell if he was hungry, but I sure didn't want his first course of the day to be possum. I looked down at Blackie as he grinned, wagging his tail. I leaned forward and petted him and he allowed it again, which was pretty great. The little possum crawled up my arm and shoulder to my hair. I was in heaven.

I hated to break the spell, but there was the weeding to do. "Go lie down, now," I said, nodding towards the house. Blackie looked behind him, and I put all my energy into sounding in charge when I said it again. "Go on."

He went, and I felt a thrill. He really was starting to listen! I put Ike down with a light heart and he followed me as I went into the field to start digging up weeds around the tomatoes. I kept a sharp eye on my little possum. He looked like he loved it out here. His nose poked inquisitively into every plant he came across, and he tried all the bugs that made their home on our squash, zucchini, and lettuce. He could have eaten the vegetables and I wouldn't have cared. I reached down for a ripe tomato, squished it in my hand, and held it out. "You like tomatoes, little guy?"

His long pink tongue darted out and tasted it, and I put it on the ground in front of him. He took another bite, then another, and then polished it off pretty neatly. He looked up at me, tongue darting out to lick the corners of his mouth.

Feeling bold, I let him try other things. Lettuce: no. Baby zucchini: yes. He gnawed on them like Blackie with a bone. The corn that peeked from under its tassels: *yes yes yes.* That was pretty funny. He chewed and chewed, little corn bits escaping from his mouth as he tried to jam more in. I loved corn too.

Just then I spotted a long green thing and jumped a mile in the air. *"Snake!"* Ike didn't jump, though. While I was still up in the air screeching, he'd already darted forward, black eyes intent on the whipcord of muscle slithering away under my feet. It was just a baby too, but I didn't care. The only good snake was a dead snake, sure as shooting.

The snake was still writhing around Ike, then all of a sudden, it went limp and I rushed forward. Ike chirped at me, his mouth rimmed with blood. I was amazed. He'd killed the snake!

Then I heaved as he started to *eat* it. "No, Ike, *no-no-no.*" I groaned. It was just too disgusting. I turned away and went back over to the innocent, blood-free squash. Blackie perked his ears and looked up as the window above him opened.

"P, you okay out there? I heard you screaming," Gran called out the window.

"I'm okay, Gran. Just thought I saw a—a snake."

She waved her hand and looked down. "Ought Blackie to be out?"

I nodded. "Yeah, he's listening to me today, and he needed some time out of his kennel." Blackie was staring at me alertly and waiting for an order. I motioned him to stay where he was, and Gran seemed to be impressed with my control over him. I know I was pretty proud of myself.

"Just keep your eyes open, all right? Goodness knows what's out there." She backed inside, shutting the window, and Blackie put his head down on his paws.

I picked up the hoe and went back to chopping. Gardening was a big pain. I dug until Ike came back over to me, *cheh-cheh*'ing, very pleased with himself. He sat up on his hind legs and started cleaning his little body. I talked to him over my shoulder as I tackled another weed. By the time I'd finished the squash, he'd finished his cleaning and was pulling on my leg, begging to be picked up. I reached down for him, putting him on my shoulder. Gran would never be able to see him from the house. He twined his fingers in my hair and sighed a little possum sigh of content.

I wondered how Dad was doing. Mama hadn't called yet to say she'd gotten there, although she'd promised. I bent down to snap off a green bean and gave it to Ike. Would they let him come home now? I knew he'd hurt his leg pretty bad before, but this second thing with the hospital bombing and extra injuries . . .

The jingle of Blackie's tags alerted me and I looked up to see a long winding trail of dirt rising off the road. "No, Blackie!" I yelled, shoving Ike down my shirt as the dog took off down the driveway. I sprinted after him.

"No!" I yelled again.

He glanced back at me as he reached the road. A truck blasted right by, flip-flopping that poor dog butt over head as it struck him.

Chapter 22

"Blackie! *Blackie!*" I raced to his side. Gran hurried off the front porch, whipping off her apron as she hobbled towards us. "What in the world? P, what happened?"

I felt sick. I'd caused this.

Blackie whimpered. He was lying all higgledy-piggledy on the side of the road. Dust covered his coat, and his back legs were twisted up and facing the wrong direction. He was panting, but stopped trying to get up when I dropped down beside him and put a hand on his head.

I swallowed my lunch back down. This couldn't be happening. "You're gonna be okay boy, you're gonna be *fine.*" I didn't realize I was saying it until I took a sobbing breath; I thought I'd just been repeating it over and over in my head. I searched for where he'd been hurt but couldn't find anything. Nothing was ripped open. His heart thundered madly under my fingers. He jerked his head like he was trying to get up, and I pushed it down with my left hand, still searching with my right. He seemed like he was hurting but I couldn't find any blood *anywhere.* How could he not get up? My heart was thudding against my chest and I couldn't breathe.

"Land a-mercy!" Gran called out.

"Call Mart's dad quick! Tell him Blackie's been hurt!" I never took my eyes off the poor dog, willing him to keep breathing.

He was panting light and quick, and a little blood trickled out of the corner of his mouth. I wiped it away with my hand and rubbed it on my shorts. "Hurry! The phone number's right by the phone. It's by 'vet.'"

She hurried off and I looked at Blackie real careful. He kept trying to get up, but his back legs—they weren't moving. I ducked my head and dried my eyes on my shirt. Blackie whimpered again and licked my arm. His whimper thrummed through me even as I touched his back legs gently. Everything was warm but very still. Not a muscle twitched. I felt so helpless, and swallowed once or twice before I could get my voice going. Oh, Blackie. "No, buddy, you're going to be okay. Just hang on." My voice cracked as I spoke.

"They're coming!" Gran called from the porch. She was wringing her hands, and crying, too. Blackie whined again and I sniffled, trying to bring my tears back under control.

"Water. Can you bring him some water?"

His eyes met mine as he panted harder. He must be in pain, I thought, and I wiped my eyes again. How could I make him more comfortable? I kept murmuring to him, my head down right by his. I looked into his odd-colored eyes, willing him to be okay. There had to be something I could do.

I gently straightened out his back legs from where they lay, willy-nilly, trying to feel if anything was working in them. They didn't seem broken, and it didn't seem to hurt him when I moved them. Was that good? I ran my finger across the bottom of his trail-roughened feet. They didn't twitch.

A truck came roaring up as Gran hurried out with water, sloshing it over the sides of the bowl in her haste. She lowered the bowl, tipping it over slightly, as close to Blackie's mouth as she could get it. I whimpered myself to see the poor dog fail to reach the water, then moved forward to support his head enough for him to lick from the side of his mouth.

The truck doors slammed and suddenly Mart and his dad were right by me. I looked up into Bill's eyes, tears streaming.

"Now, what have we here?" He was a big man with powerful arms, but his hands were light as feather down as they quickly moved across Blackie. I gulped as Mart fell to his knees beside us, him smoothing the hairs over Blackie's eyes.

"Oh, Bill, I let him out. Then a man in a green truck hit him. Then kept on! It was just an accident!" I couldn't contain my tears now, although I tried to keep my voice steady so that Blackie wouldn't get upset.

Bill's hands traveled down Blackie's back legs. He frowned and reached into his bag, pulling out his stethoscope.

"I think we saw him drive past our house." Mart kept looking between me, Blackie, and his dad with horrified eyes.

Bill sat back with a sigh, the stethoscope dangling in his hand. He looked skyward and closed his eyes briefly, and I felt my world fall down around my ears. I think I even heard the thump and crash of it, hitting that Oklahoma dirt. He didn't say anything.

"Is he . . ." Mart couldn't wait, either. He was crying like I was, water tracking down under his glasses. We both looked at his dad. Bill turned his head towards me and I looked down, not wanting to see his expression as he took a deep breath.

I finally looked up and met his eyes. Tears sparkled there and I panicked. "What's wrong? Just tell me what's wrong with him." Blackie whimpered again and I smoothed his head, scratching behind his ears. Surely Bill could fix this.

"Princess, honey," Bill said, and took a deep breath. His eyes pleaded with me to understand as he gently rested one hand on his bag and the other on our poor dog. Blackie's panting hadn't stopped; if anything, it had sped up.

"Just tell me." I was *responsible* for this.

Bill shut his eyes and opened them again. His shoulders drooped as his eyes met mine. "Blackie's got a broken back, honey. He's . . . not going to make it."

"*No!*"

I leaped up. Blackie tried to follow me, but only got his head off the ground before he yelped and let it fall back down. I collapsed next to him again, trying to keep him calm, the tears streaming down my face.

"Can't you do *something*?" Mart asked.

Bill didn't answer for a moment, then slowly shook his head. Pain spread everywhere. Everything *hurt,* more than I ever thought anything could.

Bill put his hand on his bag again, and my heart thumped crazily. He sighed. "Only one thing will help him, P. He should be put out of his misery." He pulled out a syringe and a bottle of liquid, and I sobbed, trying to control my breathing. "I need you to tell me okay."

He wanted *me* to give the okay for him to kill my dad's dog.

Bill rocked back on his heels, looking at us both. Mart had collapsed at his dad's side, his hands clenched in his jeans. I stared down at Blackie, who looked into my eyes.

I'd *almost* gotten him to be my dog. He let me pet him. He sat for me and licked me. I was gonna teach him to shake hands. I bent close to his face, still staring into his eyes—one ice-white eye and one chocolate brown. They stared back into mine, and he whimpered again, very low. I could feel it hum through his body and travel through my hands. I kissed him on his nose and he licked my lips. That was a first too.

I couldn't *not.* Swallowing hard, I looked up at Bill. "It's not going to hurt him, is it?"

"No." The vet's voice wobbled.

I laid down by my dad's dog, circling his neck with my arms and cushioning his face in my hands. My heart felt like it was melting. Blackie cleaned my tears with his tongue, panting even as he licked. "Okay then."

I laid my forehead against his, and we waited together for the end.

It didn't hurt him. I heard the hiss of the needle and felt the movement of his leg. I heard Mart sniffling. I heard Gran gasp. I heard Blackie sigh.

Then he was gone.

Chapter 23

A hand settled on my shoulder. I looked up into watery eyes almost the color of my own. Gran nodded. "You did the right thing, honey."

I couldn't speak around the lump in my throat, so I just got up and looked down at Blackie. He looked so little lying there. "I'm going to bury him." He couldn't stay out in this heat. I rubbed my hand across my eyes, stepping back from Gran.

Mart was up and beside me in a blink. "I'll help."

"Me too." His dad got up with his bag. Mart took him over to the shed where all the tools were stored.

There was really only one place that he could be buried. Every time Dad let him out of the kennel, he made a beeline for the corner of the house that had the most shade in the heat of the day. He'd already dug a nest there. It was his favorite place. I wondered for a second if my dad or mama would mind, but I just didn't care. I was responsible here, I had *done this*. I would finish it.

When Mart brought the shovel back, I pointed to where I wanted the grave to be. He carefully dug deep into the red earth, piling the soil to the side of the grave. His dad helped when Mart got tired, and I sat, watching them dig. Gran had gone back inside, after a short tug on the hair at the top of my head that made me leak some more tears. When they were done,

Bill helped me lift Blackie and place him into the hole. His head dangled when we moved him and his tongue lolled out. He looked so *dead*. "I'm so sorry," I whispered, and then I was up, fleeing towards the creek. Tears blurred my vision and weeds scratched my legs as I ran, ran, ran.

It was the worst day of my life.

Chapter 24

At the edge of the creek I bent over, my hands on my knees, gulping for breath. Sharp nails scrabbled at my skin, and I lifted Ike out with one hand, setting him gently on the ground. He snuffled around happily.

I sat there, head on my knees, crying softly for what seemed like hours. A gentle chirr, and two tiny hands touched my leg. I rubbed my eyes and looked down at Ike looking up at me, his ears pricked. I brought him up to eye level. His little hands examined my face, and when he touched my tears he pulled back, looking at his paw. He licked it, and stared at me. He reached forward again and licked my tears away. His tongue was soft against my face. Like Blackie's had been. I pulled back. "I'll be okay, bud," I said. As I headed slowly for home, Ike followed me. Baby frogs frantically jumped out of my way and Ike grabbed a couple, trying to eat them. I stopped at the water trough on the hill. The water wasn't slobbery and green-tinged, which meant I could wash my face without worrying about cow spit. I splashed halfheartedly, then sat down on the edge of the trough and stared at the ground.

I watched Ike finishing off another baby frog and frowned. Staying around me was just plain dangerous, especially for animals I loved. I'd have to try to get Ike settled in the wild as soon as I could. He needed to get away from me, before something bad happened to him, too.

I straightened my back and clenched my fists. Ike was going to learn how to live away from humans quick, and I was going to teach him. We'd just have to step up his possum training.

"Time to go back, buddy." I got up and started walking, half turning to look back at him. He was following, leaping over tufts of grass I never even noticed as I went along. Tail poked straight out behind him, he'd run and hop as fast as he could until he got caught up, and then he'd get sidetracked again. He slowed a little when we were about halfway home and finally stopped, chittering at me. It was farther than he'd ever walked by himself, and I was proud of how long he'd gone on his own. I went back and stuck him in my shirt, where he settled right down, curling up and becoming very still. I thought perhaps I'd need to wear a baggier shirt. Ike was getting bigger and I looked like Sally, the only girl in my class who'd "blossomed" last year.

Dust on the road caught my attention, and I followed it from where I stood. *Great.* Joe's truck was coming over. I slowed down. My gran gave him the heebie-jeebies, and he usually made tracks as soon as he realized she was there. Maybe he'd be gone by the time I got home if I walked real slow. But as I rounded the corner of the barn heading into the main corral, I knew it hadn't worked.

I kept my eyes firmly away from the freshly turned earth by the house and went around to the front. They were there on the porch, drinking coffee and looking in the general direction of Blackie's grave. I swallowed. "Hey, Joe. Gran." My voice didn't sound normal, but at least I wasn't crying. I swallowed again, avoiding their eyes. "You here for the cattle, Joe? Everyone's all right. You can go on home." I quickly moved past them, sliding into the house before he could answer. Then I shut the door and leaned my ear up against it. I didn't want to talk to him, but I sure wanted to hear what he was saying.

"She's taking it real hard." His voice was low, and his dusty boots creaked as he shifted on the cement.

"It happened before her eyes, Joe. Wouldn't you be a little

broke up?" Gran didn't mention why Blackie had been out, and I loved her that second more than I ever had my whole life.

He didn't say anything for a minute, and then I heard him clear his throat. "Well. I didn't come here tonight for the cattle dog."

"No?"

"Naw. There's rabies going round, real bad."

I shut my eyes. If I wasn't careful, she'd never let me out of her sight, much less down to the river bottoms. Joe needed to be quiet.

"Rabies?"

"Been carrying this gun around. Done shot two raccoons what had it just today, and I reckon a badger that was pretty far gone. Tell P to be careful out there. Any animal moves or looks funny at her, starts chasing her, tell her to run and not look back. *Do not let it near her*, hear?"

I shut my eyes. I was doomed.

"Tell her to be careful." There was a pause. "Tell her I'm real sorry for the dog, too." He clomped off the porch and I lit out for my room.

Gran knocked softly on the bedroom door, opened it a crack. "How you doing, honey?"

"I can't believe he's gone, Gran. It was all my fault. Mine." My eyes filled.

Before I knew what was what she was sitting by me, holding my hand and rubbing my back. Her hand paused over the outline of the sports bra but she didn't say anything. Just to be sure, I stiffened up a little and pulled back, sniffling, and wiped my nose with my arm. She pulled a tissue from her apron with a sigh, and handed it to me. "Use this, you rascal." She swallowed. "Fish-stick, it's always hard when an animal we love dies. You wonder why it happened, and if the universe is just out to get you. You've just got to trust it happened for a reason, and try not to think about how he was . . . at the end." Blackie's eyes pleading with me flashed into my mind, and I shook my head a little.

She grabbed my chin and forced me to look at her. She tried to smile; it wobbled around the sides of her mouth but didn't make it fully to her face. "You did all you could've done, P." At my deep sigh, she nodded. "I know it's not easy right now. But it will get easier." She dropped my chin and I rubbed it. Gran had a grip of pure steel. "Why did you let Blackie out of that cage?" She watched me closely. I looked down and away.

"I wanted him to be my friend, Gran. I'd only let him out a couple other times."

She sat there a moment, thinking, then slapped her hands on her knees and got up. "Forgiving yourself won't happen overnight, sweetheart. But you do need to do it." She tipped her head to the side. "Try to get some sleep."

Chapter 25

Somehow, the days passed. Mama had called and said that Dad was on the mend, even the new injuries, and they'd be home as soon as they could. Everyone was being nice to me. Gran cooked my favorite meals and baked cookies, rich and dark with chocolate chips, to try to make me feel better. Mart brought me a book on possums. Gran even let me continue to go on down to the bottoms, so Ike training was able to continue.

Even Mon tried. She'd corralled me in my room just today, after she gave me some time, I guess.

"Look, do you want one? Another dog? Tucker's dog just had babies. . . ." Her voice angled off as she looked into my furious eyes. I couldn't just replace Blackie for Dad, just like that! That wasn't how it worked!

"Nope. I can't have a pet, remember?" I stood up and opened the door, staring at her and nodding in its direction. "Do you mind?"

"We can talk about it if you want," she huffed, but I shook my head.

"Thanks, Mon, but no."

Some things helped, like Ike's bright possum face in the mornings. Some things didn't help, like having to write to my dad about killing his dog. I'd written the letter and Gran had sent it. It had taken me a long time to write it. I was as honest as I could be.

Dad—

I'm sorry. I let Blackie out and he chased a truck and got killed. I didn't mean for it to happen, and I'm really sad about it. I'm really sorry.

Love P.

He hadn't answered me, although Mon had gotten a letter from him since I'd sent it. He was mad at me, sure as shooting. To make it worse, I couldn't sleep. Blackie's final moments were with me all the time. Somehow, his death had entered my lightning nightmare. Now the lightning jumped from cow to cow, and Dad gave me the gun as Blackie got hit too. The new part—the lightning going away and Blackie, bloody, writhing around on the ground—would bring me awake, gasping.

It was dinnertime, but I wasn't very hungry. I sat in my room, staring out the window as Ike snuffled under the bed. While I sat there, nighttime had come. Oklahoma was funny that way. You'd have sun and sun and sun all day right up until late, and then *boom!*—the night suddenly took over.

I looked down to find Ike crawling up the side of the bed. I watched him until he'd snuggled down into his bed of pillows, and thought about tomorrow. I'd need to make a list for our training . . . and would have to talk to Mart. . . . I sat back against the headboard and thought about what training would happen next . . .

. . . and sat up in bed with a start, staring around wildly.

It wasn't even my nightmare what woke me. There'd been a scream that ended in a sneeze. It was completely dark in my room—except for a shaft of light from the door. My door was cracked open. It was *never* open.

I leaped up in a panic and shut it, looking around, under and over everything. I'd fallen asleep?

"Ike, *Ike!*" I snapped on the light and looked all over. No dice. He wasn't there.

Another scream. *Monica.* I flung open my door and raced to

my sister's room. The light was on. Mon stood on her tip-toes on top of her bed, screeching her fool head off and staring down at my possum. I gasped.

Ike lay on the floor, motionless. I rushed over to him. "Ike!" I yelled. His eyes were glassy. I lifted him up to my ear, holding my breath until I felt the faint whiffs of air from his nose stir my hair. He was breathing. What was wrong with him? His mouth gaped open and he was stiff and still. He even stank a little.

"Ike? *Ike?*" My sister yelled behind me, but I just ignored her.

Then I got it. My sister had scared him to death. He was playing possum.

Monica was still squealing like a stuck pig. I felt my stomach drop as Gran appeared at the doorway in her curlers and nightdress with a face like thunder. "What have we here, Princess Renee Miller? Monica, stop that caterwauling." Gran's voice was cold and I got real antsy. "Gran, he—I—um." I just looked mutely back at her. She walked slowly into the room, eyes trained on my poor possum. I clutched him to me.

"Princess, is this *yours?*"

My mind was running in circles. I didn't know what to do. Own up to it? Not? I caught a glimpse of Mon, staring at me intently. She'd shut up when Gran came in. I took a deep breath. "No. Well, yes. I mean, he's mine." I cradled him against my chest. "Blackie . . ." I sniffed, then continued. "Blackie killed his mother. I promised him I would get him big enough to be okay in the bottoms and then I'd let him go. I promised him!" I stared from Gran to Monica, trying to make them understand as Ike stirred. "He's never hurt anybody! He's my friend!"

Mon snorted. "He could have given me rabies and he was *in my room!*" Her voice jumped an octave with each word before she sneezed hard enough to flatten her hair.

"How long have you had him?" Gran's voice was quiet, but that didn't change the intensity or the dark tone of disapproval in it.

"Since a week before school ended."

"What?" Gran's voice rose at the end, like she didn't believe me. I bristled. "What did you do during school?"

"Why, I took him."

"How?" Her eyes were saucers.

Now I was *really* going to get it. I glanced at Monica, waiting for the explosion as I lifted up my shirt with one hand, still cradling Ike in my other. "In this."

"My *bra!*" Mon's voice rang out. Her face flushed like a cherry pie dropped on white tile. "You stupid—my—my *bra!* How did you get it?" Mon was so mad her voice had quieted down to a whisper.

I shrugged. "It wasn't that hard. Out of your dresser."

"You went through my *things?*" She sneezed again. "Am I allergic to this possum? Is this why I've been sneezing?" Her hands curled into fists.

Gran got between us before Mon could jump me.

"I needed something to be able to keep him with me. It was perfect." Gran snorted. Mon's face was puce red, and she started to get off the bed.

"Why, you little—"

I backed up, fast-talking my way out of her room with a hand raised in front of me. "Look, how was my door open? My door is never open. You'd *still* not know about him if it wasn't for that. I'd kept him hidden this long!" There was no way Mon had gone in my room—but if she hadn't, who had? Why?

"That was me," Gran said. She looked down at her hands, and then back at me. "You'd been . . . so upset from Blackie and what happened. I've been checking on you, in the night. I must have left it open, but how could I have known you were harboring a wild animal in your room?"

Wild animal? I checked that Ike was back to himself again, then walked over to Gran. She shrank back. "What, this? A wild animal? He's just a baby, Gran." Ike hissed at her, but that wasn't surprising. He'd hissed at Mart, too. I petted him. He hid his head under my hand and I looked up at Gran. "I'm all he's got."

Gran wavered, I saw it.

"If I let him loose now, he'll die." My voice was certain and sure.

"No!" Monica stood up too and walked to the right of me, standing to face Gran. "I don't want to be a part of what will happen if Dad finds out!"

Gran looked puzzled, and I blushed.

"If your dad finds out?" Gran asked, looking at Monica. "What do you mean?" I pulled Ike to my chest, cupping my hands around him to protect him from what I knew Monica was going to say.

"Dad—she's not supposed to have any pets! She promised Dad before he left!" She was almost babbling now. "She shouldn't've been messing with Blackie, and she shouldn't have that rat there!"

"Fishstick, is this true?"

"Technically, yes."

She sighed and looked away from us both. I waited, stroking Ike, his face turned up to me. When I stopped petting, he nudged me with his head and nose to remind me he was there.

"Well." She looked at me, her face serious. "Do you think you can really get this possum trained up? You think you'll be able to let him go? He's a wild animal in the end, not a pet."

Mon gasped.

I nodded, hoping . . . waiting. "Gran, I've been training him now for a couple weeks, down in the bottoms." She fiddled with her curlers and I stood still as a mouse. What would I do if she said no? Could she be the boss of me? What if I had to defy my very own gran?

"You've got two weeks."

I blinked. Mon groaned. "What?"

"Two weeks to get him ready to go. He needs to be gone before your father and mother get back. That's the time you've got." She leveled a glare at me. "Enough?"

It would have to be. I nodded slowly, fighting the urge to squeeze Ike until he squeaked. We had two weeks.

"*What?* She keeps a wild animal in the house and she doesn't even get in trouble?" Mon's mouth was hanging open now.

"It's my decision, young lady. And you are not to breathe a word of it to your parents either, hear?" Gran glared until Mon nodded, sullen.

I had to know. "Are *you* going to tell Mama and Dad?"

"Not until they come home. *After*"—Gran stared at me— "your possum is gone." She took another deep breath and smiled. "What's his name, Fishstick?"

"Ike."

Gran looked at me funny. "You named him after your gramps?" I nodded, and she shook her head, looking down. "We've got to get you out more."

I watched her turn around and leave the room. I headed for mine—to go to sleep so that I could call Mart first thing. I had to get cracking, and I needed his help. I had only two weeks.

Chapter 26

The next morning, Ike was back to normal and busy exploring under the bed with an occasional sneeze. It was dusty under there. I left him in my room and went to call Mart.

"Mart, it's me."

"What's going on?"

"Gran found out about Ike." At his gasp, I hurried to explain. "It's okay—she's given me two weeks to get him good enough to be let go. What do you think, did your Internet stuff say anything about when they can be set free?"

I heard the clicking over the phone as he started to type. "Wow, your gran found out. And she didn't tan you?"

"Nope. Even Mon knows."

"Wow." He was quiet a minute more, but the tapping sound continued. I just sat and let him type. The computer beeped and he sighed.

"Well, he's able to be let out relatively quickly after being out of his mama's pouch, roughly seven inches long. Can you measure him?"

"They go by measurement?" I eyeballed my possum from where I sat, but couldn't tell how long he was. I'd have to check. He was exploring inside my tennis shoe, and his long hairless tail draped over the side.

"Evidently." Mart's voice was dry.

"Hold on." I headed back to my mama and dad's room. I knew she had a flexible ruler in her sewing basket. I hoped Gran wasn't in there to ask me what I was doing messing with Mama's sewing things. She wasn't.

You could tell my dad hadn't been there in a while. His dresser was a shrine—his cologne was still in its spot, and his wallet and keys and stuff still lay strewn across the top. It looked like he could walk in at any moment.

I grabbed the ruler from Mama's sewing basket and ran back to my room. "Hold on, I found something to measure. It'll take a minute." I tossed the phone onto the bed and grabbed my tennis shoe. Ike had made that his favorite place recently, and he didn't like the idea of coming out. He dug his claws in, but I finally got him out by wiggling a finger underneath his pudgy belly as he hissed in irritation. He was real antsy, wriggling around like a worm on a hook as I tried to make him be still. Even though he was twitching something fierce, I managed to mark his little body, without tail, at seven and a half inches long. I petted his head as he hissed at me. When I let him go, he waddled to my shoe again.

"He's seven and a half inches, Mart."

"Well, you said you had how long?"

"Two weeks."

"Two weeks should be enough."

"Look, does your dad still have that tent you told me about?" Bill kept trying to make his family interested in the Great Outdoors, as he called it, but nobody was.

"I think so. Why?" Mart was a very suspicious person.

I rolled my eyes and tried to make my voice sound hurt. "Why are you so suspicious? I just want to invite you—"

"No."

"To come with me and Ike—"

"No."

"Down to the river once, overnight."

"No."

"Like, tomorrow."

"*No.*"

"Come on. It's not going to kill you."

"P, I *don't camp.*"

"One night? Come on, Mart, it's important." I paused, and when he didn't say anything, I said, "It would really help me. Please?" The silence on the other end of the line stretched on and on.

After a while Mart sighed. "Fine." His voice sounded glum.

I didn't give him a chance to change his mind. "Great, then. What do you say, about nine-ish?" He sighed. "You'll bring the tent?" He humphed at me. "*And* the blankets and stuff?" He snorted.

"What are *you* bringing?"

"The possum."

"What about your gran? What does she say?"

"She said as long as it's both of us it's okay." I smiled, imagining him rolling his eyes.

"Fine."

I hung up. Now I could teach Ike what to do at night when you were a possum. I got up and went to pack my backpack, and then took Ike outside to practice catching snails.

Mart drove up on his four-wheeler the next evening. "Ready?"

I couldn't believe what I was seeing. "Jeez Louise. Are *you*?" He was dressed for the Arctic, not a simple night out under the Oklahoma stars. He had on a puffy jacket, jeans with hiking boots, for crying out loud, and his glasses were surrounded by some larger goggle thing that made him look cross-eyed.

He snorted at me. "I'm just prepared."

Whatever. I got on the four-wheeler after opening the honeycomb gates and he drove inside as we headed for the creek in our pasture. The tent eventually bounced into view, lit by the headlights. "You already set it up?" Mart asked.

"No, your dad came by earlier." It had been child's play for

Bill to talk Gran into it. She thought he hung the moon since the whole Blackie incident. I couldn't see Mart's face past the goggle thing, but I thought he was frowning.

"Figures," he said, and I didn't say anything else. His dad had probably cried tears of joy when Mart asked to use the tent. "I bet he bought us some snacks, too." He unzipped the door flap and I must have made a crazy sound when I looked inside because he snorted again. "Haven't you seen food before?" His voice was little and snippy, but I forgave him. I crawled in and drooled at the haul. Corn chips and chocolate cookie packages were stacked against one side of the tent. Warm spicy smells coming from a covered container hinted we had burritos for supper, and a cooler stood next to the chips. I opened it. Soda pop!

I turned and beamed at Mart. "Man, when your dad does something, he doesn't do it halfway, does he?"

The couple times we'd gone camping as a family, we'd been stuck with some gross ham sandwiches, soggy potato chips, and tap water. And our sleeping bags were thin. I looked at the two air mattresses and waggled my eyebrows at Mart. He took off his goggle things and glanced back at me.

"This kind of thing makes you *happy?*"

As we unpacked and got ready for the night, I let Ike out of my shirt. He waddled around us, getting in the way, until I fed him a corn chip. Then another. Then I turned to help set up the rest of the tent and he got real quiet. After I hadn't heard whisker or tail for some time I looked around for him. The chip bag made a noise.

"Ike!" He was inside it, making fast and furious crunching sounds. Mart laughed and laughed and I did too, although I was still a little put out. I *never* got to eat chips, and that crazy possum got an entire bag to himself. Mart tore open another bag, grabbing a handful as he passed it to me. "Have some! And set up the lantern."

The battery-powered lantern threw its feeble light in a small circle around us. Ike was busy cleaning himself after his corn

chip buffet. Mart was lying on one air mattress; I'd claimed the other. He crossed his hands over his chest, the soda pop can beside him glistening with water drops in the lamplight. "He said we can keep the tent here as long as we want. This isn't that bad," he said, almost under his breath. "If it's just like this then I can handle it."

I laughed. I'd only camped a couple times, but in my experience, it wasn't often like this. Ike chirred and I unzipped the door flap, letting him out. "This *is* nice," I agreed. We laid on the mattresses and listened to the sounds of the night over the crunches of nacho-cheese-flavored chips. Crickets were chirping, the cicadas were whirring, and somewhere a cow was mooing.

"Do you ever feel like your dad wants something out of you?" Mart suddenly said, his voice hardly louder than the sounds outside. I struggled to swallow a gigantic mouthful of chips.

"Yeah." I stared up at the ceiling. The moon shone softly through the fabric, but not enough to be bright. A friendly sort of shining. "Usually I just think he's not happy with me, though. Do you?"

The air mattress creaked. "He wants me to help him with the vet stuff, not 'play with the computer all day.'" He sighed and I inhaled softly, the plastic smell of the air mattress sneaking into my nose. It was the first time Mart had ever mentioned stuff between him and his dad. "I don't know what he wants from me."

"Maybe he just wants to share the things he likes with you—like camping and stuff," I offered.

Ike snuffled his way back inside and made his slow, careful way to my arm. He checked to make sure I was still there, prowled around the tent a moment, then left again.

There was a sound in the darkness, like a hand slapping the ground in anger. Mart snorted. The sounds outside stilled, except for the cow. It kept mooing. Cows mooed all the time, though. Moo, eat, and poop. It's what they did.

"Maybe you're right," Mart said. His shadow moved as he sat up. "I have to go to the bathroom. Where's the TP?"

I goggled at him. "TP? Toilet paper?" It was my turn to snort. "What do you think this is, a hotel? It's drip-dry, buddy, or use some leaves."

"I can't—*drip-dry*! Leaves?" He sounded horrified and hopped up and down as he danced from foot to foot. "Come on, P, I really have to *go*. Where is it?"

I sat up. "Mart, I'm not kidding. I don't have any. Use some leaves, I tell ya!" He darted for the door. "Off a tree!" I bellowed to his retreating back. Giggling softly, I listened to him crashing away.

What was *wrong* with that cow? I sat up, frowning, and looked outside. It should've shut up by now.

Mart crashed his way back and poked his head inside the tent.

"Done?"

"Shut up. Bring the lantern, would ya?"

"Why?" I stowed Ike on top of my head as I reached for the lantern.

"Just come on."

I followed him through the darkness, mystified. The mooing kept getting louder and louder until it sounded like we were right on top of it. Mart grabbed me and pulled me behind one of the cottonwoods right by the river. He pointed at a shadow in the darkness. "Look at that cow. Is that normal?"

Chapter 27

I looked. It was Loosygoosy and she *was* acting funny. She kept walking in a circle, her head down. Every once in a while she'd tilt her head straight back and force out a moo around whatever seemed to be strangling her. The sound was raspier up close— little and tinny and *forced*, most of all. Her calf followed her, trying to nurse but not being able to get a nose under before Loosy'd walk off again, staggering slightly. Once she circled closer to us, I could see that she was drooling.

"Crap!" I ducked behind the tree, pulling Mart back with me.

"What?" he whispered. I braced my hands against the tree trunk and just shook for a moment. He grabbed my shoulder with one hand and scratched the other hand against his jeans. He turned and rubbed against the tree trunk, making a sound of relief as he scrubbed.

The shaking in my hands seemed like it'd gone farther down to my stomach. I felt cold all over, and felt like my hair was standing on end. Ike reached for the tree and I let him go, pushing him up onto the first branch. I turned to Mart. "Mart, get up in the tree with Ike. *Get up!*" He opened his mouth to argue but I cut him off. "It's Loosy. I think she might have rabies." His mouth shut like a turtle's, *whomp*, and he started up, tripping over himself to climb faster. I shoved on his rear a little, helping him get a foothold higher in the tree. The flashlight he'd been carrying dropped right onto my head, and I stopped pushing him to grab my noggin with both hands, groaning. "Ow!" The lantern fell out of my hands, landed on its side, and went out.

The moo came again, but lower.

"P!" Mart called out, screeching, and I looked around the cottonwood tree to see the cow coming at me full force. Her eyes glinted red in the light.

I made a break for the nearest big tree that I could duck behind. Hiding there, I watched as she stumbled by with her head down. She wasn't mooing so much now. She was making a long protracted groan, and slobber boiled from her mouth as she hobbled quickly past like a cow zombie.

. I flinched as she crashed into another tree with her head, the melon-crack sound making me jump. She didn't seem to be able to stop herself or control her movements, but she sure was furious. I didn't stop to see if she'd get up. I zipped around the tree, snagged the flashlight, and leaped for a handhold, fearing the sound of Loosy's head crashing into me from below. Mart hooked my shoulder with one arm and heaved as I scrabbled. Ike chirred above me.

"Hurry . . . hurry," Mart cried as I grabbed at branches and vines, pulling myself up as quickly as I could. I turned to look at him.

"Watch out!" Mart shouted as the cow slammed into our tree, rattling the cottonwood leaves as our branch swayed dangerously. Leaves drifted down around us as she looked up, bellowing harshly. The flashlight quivered in my hand. A cracking sound seemed to be coming from inside the tree. That couldn't be good. If the branch broke we'd be under her hooves and her slobber. I raced through possibilities in my head as Mart sat and shook behind me, alternatively scratching his hand and his rear. I couldn't handle his twitching anymore.

"Why are you scratching like that?" I asked, thinking about how we were gonna get out of this pickle.

"Look at my hand!" he whispered angrily, shoving it into the glow of the flashlight. I moved the light and the cow chased it, head down and bellowing her madness. She followed the light track on the ground. That might help. . . . I looked down at Mart's hand. It was red, and small blisters were popping up on it. "Where did you go to the bathroom?" I asked him, handing him the flashlight. "Point to it." He did, and the flashlight settled on a thicker huddle of baby cottonwoods, their trunks covered by bright red leaves.

I had a crazy urge to burst out laughing, but I tried to steady my voice. "Mart, did you use the red leaves on the trunk or the green leaves on the tree itself?"

"The red ones. You said use the leaves on the tree. I could reach those." He nodded and I let my forehead fall into my palm with a thud. "Why?"

"You used them to wipe? *Everywhere?*"

"Yes! Now tell me why!" His voice was already panicky, but when I didn't say anything it rose a few notes to where he could be singing with gran if he had a mind to. "What's *wrong?*"

I couldn't hold it in anymore. I laughed until I was hoarse. Every time I caught sight of his face it set me off again, till he was as red as a tomato and as mad as a hornet. I couldn't look at him or I'd be off again. And I had to think about what to do with the cow.

"Mart, by the sound of it, you've got poison ivy. You used the red leaves to *wipe* with. Your rear, I mean. You must be allergic to it."

"But . . . I touched you!"

"I'm not allergic. It doesn't affect me." He looked at his hand with a visible shudder.

The cow came back, and the shaking of the tree as she plowed into it sobered me right up. I took a deep breath. "Look. We've got to do something about this cow." I hiccuped, swallowing hard. I'd have to try to tie her with the rope I had in my backpack so we could get down. I couldn't handle Gran coming to look for us tomorrow morning with *that* on the loose.

"I brought some rope with me to train Ike to climb trees. It's back in the tent. What we're going to have to do is—we need to get her tied to a tree, and for that, we need to get her attention away from us." I gritted my teeth as the tree whipped back and forth from the power of yet another blow. A bone-deep grinding sound came from below me, and I knew we didn't have much time.

"Look. See this?" I pointed the flashlight and the enraged cow lumbered after the bright ball of light on the ground. "She keeps following that light. You need to keep her chasing that while I get the rope. *Do it*," I said, shoving the flashlight into his hand. "Keep it going, don't let her remember me, okay?" I looked down at her as she stumbled into another tree. Her calf moped along behind her, ears drooping as he called for her. It made me sick. This was the first animal I'd seen alive with rabies. Poor cow.

"Keep her moving, Mart." He nodded weakly as I dropped to the ground and made for the tent.

I followed her crashing sounds in the darkness as I dug through my backpack, then gave up and took the whole thing with me. I finally grabbed the strong rawhide rope and looked around for a suitable tree. As Loosy lumbered past chasing the light, I darted to a tree a little farther away, running around it twice before tying a heavy knot. I threw my weight against it, freezing in terror as she tottered past again only to double back a moment later.

The rope would hold. I grabbed the other end and tied a thick double-sided knot in it. I held the circle in my hands, thought about that crazy cow's head coming through it, and took a deep breath. "Mart! Put the light about a couple feet away from me here, okay?" The wild crashes of the cow grew louder as she came towards me. She was focused on the white ball that bobbed right by her hooves, and she was bawling something fierce. Her slobber marked the ground along her crazy path, and I hoped it wouldn't get on me.

"Now stop it! And don't move it for anything, hear?" I called, and he yelled back an okay. I peeked around the trunk and saw her drop to her knees, the rabies making her clumsy, and grind her head into the ground where the light had stopped.

I took a deep breath and stepped around the tree.

"No! P!" Mart screamed, but it was too late. Quick as a thought I ran up to her and shouted. She looked up from the ground and my knees wavered, but then I had that loop around her neck before she knew what I was doing. I didn't know how long she'd have to run before the rope ran out, so I turned and busted outta there. I could hear her hot on my trail, and I could hear Mart puking up the remains of his corn chips as I ran. I kept running even when I heard a sort of whoop sound. Ducking behind a tree, I waited for her to fly past.

She didn't.

Mart's yell of victory confirmed that I'd done it. She was tied. I sank down to the ground, my legs too weak to hold me.

There was a loud crunch and I looked back to see Loosy demolishing the flashlight. "Hey!" I screeched, jumping up and looking wildly around. "Mart!"

"Over here!" I turned around to see him holding my backpack in one hand and Ike in the other. The little possum was hissing up a storm, and I ran over to take him from Mart.

"Good job," I said, looking at him a second before staring at the cow as she finished off my dad's favorite flashlight. Ike scrambled up the side of my head, muttering and hissing the whole time.

"Thanks. I thought she could have the flashlight for letting us live." His face was flushed but he was smiling. I looked past the vomit on his shirt and smiled back.

"Um, I don't know about you, but," I said, as I turned back towards home and he scratched himself furiously, "I vote we call this a night. Let's not take the four-wheeler, it's too slow."

We hurried back to the house, Loosy's bellows echoing behind us.

Chapter 28

The house was silent when we entered, but not for long. I flipped on the kitchen light as I blasted through, Mart hard on my heels. When we reached the hall he split off for the bathroom while I continued down to Mama and Dad's room. "Use some lotion! It'll help!" I called over my shoulder.

"Gran! *One of the cows has rabies and almost got us and I tied her up and almost got it and we had to run through the dark here to tell you and Mart has poison ivy on his butt and he can't stop scratching it!*" It was pitch black in the room, and I turned the light on in time to see Gran come boiling up from underneath the covers, the curls on her head askew. I was hopping up and down in my haste, Ike bobbing on my head like the toy man in a jack-in-the-box. His irate chitterings only added to the craziness in the room.

"Wha-what?"

As I opened my mouth to say it all again, she shook her head. "One sentence at a time, please. And inhale between them."

After a deep breath, I started again. "Loosygoosy was moo-ing." Breath. "She was drooling." Breath. "When I got outside to check on her she ran at me." Breath. "I think she has rabies." Breath. I perked up. "Oh, hold on!" I shuffled through my back-pack and pulled out my Lookbook.

"Remember?" I said as I scanned the pages. "She had a cut on her leg, and there were lots of flies on it." I found the entry from some weeks back. "She's been acting funny," I said, dog-earing the pages as I flipped through them, "but I didn't know she had rabies. I just thought she was irritated by the sore leg or something. We need to call the vet." Gran's eyes were gray and rheumy, but she seemed to get the gist of the problem now. She opened her mouth.

"Already did." Mart said from behind me, the cordless phone in his hand. "Dad's on his way."

Gran looked over at him and reached for her glasses. "Young man," she said, staring at him. "Did my granddaughter just inform me you have poison ivy on your rear appendage?" I fell back against the wall to giggle as Mart turned a violent shade of purple. He looked down and nodded. "How did *that* happen?" Mart was spared having to answer, 'cause his dad's truck lights swung into the driveway. Gran ducked back underneath the covers.

"Land a-mercy, what's next?" I heard her mutter. I stuck Ike in my shirt as I followed Mart out the door.

His dad was still wearing his pajama top, which made me giggle. "Kids? What's going on here? P, Mart said something about a rabid cow attacking you in your pasture?" He looked from Mart to me, and I nodded. His dark blond hair was sticking up on one side, and his clothes were rumpled.

"Sorry to wake you up, sir, but Loosygoosy—that's one of our cows—did try to get us. She was following the flashlight that Mart was moving." Mart puffed up his chest. "Then we tied her up and came home."

"What? Where's the flashlight then? How did you tie her up?" At this, Mart's chest deflated.

"Um, the cow got the flashlight."

"And, ah . . ." I looked down and over at Mart. "She ran through a loop of rope we made that we tied to a tree." Mart was staring up at his dad now, and I drooped my shoulders in relief. I knew we'd get a hiding if he knew the real story. He was staring at us like he didn't quite believe us.

"Her calf is real upset—"

"She has a calf?" He asked as he jogged to the back of his truck. He rooted around, pulling out his doctor bag and a long narrow black thing.

"Yup, some months old. If she does have rabies, can the calf get it?"

He didn't even answer me, just nodded at us, motioning towards the truck.

"P, open the gates and shut them behind us. Mart, get in the truck and explain how a rabid cow got a flashlight you were holding." He gave Mart a short hug before tossing him up into the truck like a bag of corn. I jumped in, too. We were through them and bumping across the pasture before he spoke again.

"What's that smell?" I hadn't noticed it—a light flowery smell like the lotions Mon and Mama used after showering. It did smell out of place.

Mart shifted in his seat. "Lotion," he mumbled. His dad huffed some air out and glanced at him as he drove along. I shoved my fist into my mouth.

"Lotion? What were you guys *doing*?"

"It was the only kind in the bathroom," Mart muttered, still staring at his hands. I could feel the heat from his face coming off him in waves, so I decided to answer for him.

"Um, Mart got poison ivy. He was just using the lotion on it."

"Poison ivy?" Bill looked at his son, who sank down even deeper in the seat, staring at his hands. "Where?"

"My hand . . . and my rear end." You almost couldn't hear that last part, and I laughed under my breath, looking out the window.

We drove the last little way before Bill said anything, and then that was just a sigh. "You two . . . honestly."

When Bill turned off the engine, we heard Loosy mooing. Bill shook his head and opened the door. I cracked my side but he stopped and looked back at us both. He held up a hand and pointed a finger at us. "If I tell you to get into the truck, I want you to do it right away, hear me? No arguments." He frowned at both of us and we nodded. Bill picked up his doctor's bag and a rifle. I shuddered.

When we got up closer to her I knew I had been right. Something was definitely wrong with the cow. She hadn't seen us yet, and was swaying and bawling. Slobber spattered the ground under her.

Bill set down his bag and crept behind a tree to watch her. I shifted my feet, uncomfortable, and the cow saw me. Immediately she began straining at the rope. Her eyes bulged, white rims separating the brown irises from the darkness of her face, making her look even crazier. Bill snuck back over to me. She saw him and twisted towards him in her rage, pulling against the rope for all she was worth. He leaned against the tree. "Mart said the cow had a cut?" Bill asked.

I nodded. "A couple weeks back she had some punctures on her leg. She could walk on it and everything, so I didn't call you. It healed okay, but then she started to act weird." He was silent. "Do you . . . think that's what she has?"

"I think she just might. Those slashes could have been an animal bite, and I've had it happen with cows before. She's just . . . expensive. Your dad isn't here."

I didn't see his problem. "So? You're saying she's dangerous right now?"

"Very. She can't live like that." He snorted and motioned to her. She'd dropped her head and was swaying back and forth, bellowing slowly. Every time anything moved she was on it, straining towards it with all her strength, mooing crazily.

I could see his point. "So what's the problem?"

"P, the problem is that she is an expensive cow and it's more than likely she *is* rabid, and if so, I'm going to have to put her down." At my gasp, he nodded. "You see? Not a responsibility I'm eager to take on."

It wasn't *his* responsibility. *I* was in charge. I poked him in the side and looked him in the eyes. "Bill, while my dad's gone, *I'm* in charge of this farm." I paused while he looked at me. "Not you, not Joe, not Gran. If you think she has rabies, then we have to put her down."

I pointed at the gun. "You going to do it, or shall I?" I had a flashback to my nightmare and my dad shaking his head before handing me the gun. Was this what he'd been trying to tell me?

"I'll do it, Princess."

He walked around the tree to face the cow. As she started pulling at the end of the rope, I closed my eyes. But I still heard the shot—and the thud as she fell.

Ike exploded out of my shirt with a force that surprised me. I could hardly hold him as he twisted in my hands like a wet fish, hissing and chittering for all he was worth. I'd forgotten he had such a fear of guns. As Bill turned around I ran off in the other direction, frantically holding the possum and trying to make myself look normal from behind. Ike's eyes were huge and black in the dimness, his mouth white and wide open, hissing wildly. His nails scraped down my hands as he struggled to get away.

"P? *Princess?*"

"In a minute!" I called back, desperate, Ike's body a gigantic fluff ball in my sweating hands. "I'm going to the bathroom!"

"Watch the leaves you use!" he said, laughing, and I could hear Mart snort.

It took me some time to get Ike settled down. I had to do a lot of petting and murmuring before I could shove him down my shirt and meet Mart and Bill by the cow.

"Better?" Mart asked me, his glasses glinting in the moonlight.

"Yeah." A slight hiss from my chest emphasized my answer, and Mart snorted again.

Ike hissed the whole way home, his body tense and hard against my chest. His nose pointed out of my shirt towards Bill as if the shot had made him the enemy now.

As I lay in my bed, Ike a warm weight beside me, I thought about Loosy. We'd left her lying where she was; Bill said he'd get his helpers out tomorrow to bring her to the lab so he could test her blood and brains, but he was pretty sure she had rabies. He'd lassoed the calf and it was staying at his barn for the night.

I flipped over on my side, staring at the wall. *Another* one of Dad's animals dead while I was in charge.

I watched as Ike burrowed his way into his pile of pillows. Mart told me that possums rarely get it, luckily. Something about their blood temperature being lower than that of other mammals.

I rubbed my feet together under the covers, remembering how Bill had gone over my feet before he left, checking for cuts that could let the rabies virus in. He hadn't found any, but . . .

The dream was different again that night, and I shuddered as the lightning traced across the sky in a mad buildup before the striking began. The cows, Blackie, my dad . . . but when the thunder cracked, I saw Ike there, staring up at me and Dad, and I had the gun in my hand. I lost my grip on the nightmare and shot awake with a start. "Oh no, oh no," I gasped, digging through the pillows and holding my possum close to me. He struggled a bit, not understanding, so I put him down.

The door cracked and I saw Gran in her curlers peek in. "Honey, you all right? I heard you screaming." She flipped the light on and must have seen something in my face because she hobbled inside quick, sitting on the edge of the bed. "What's going on, Fishstick?" Her warm blue eyes stared at me.

"It's these nightmares, Gran. Bad ones," I said, glancing at her out of the corner of my eye. "Everybody's dying in them—animals, people. . . . I'm afraid." I took a deep breath.

Ike climbed up onto my side and hissed at Gran. After a moment, she patted my foot.

"You've had a terrible fright tonight. It's no wonder you're upset." I sniffed, and Gran ruffled the hair on the top of my head. "I'll stay here till you fall asleep," she said.

It took a long time.

Chapter 29

As I looked out over the creek down by our house, I figured I'd done everything I could. Ike sat on my head, looking at the sweeping yellow grasses, the drooping cottonwoods and their vine-covered trunks. I felt my backpack for the bulge I knew contained enough food for Ike in case he couldn't find it on his own right away.

Today was the day. Time to let him go.

I'd practiced and practiced for this moment. We'd spent more nights out here—but without Mart. He was just completely turned off by the idea of camping. I couldn't even get him on the phone, he was so disgusted.

I'd gone alone and slept in the tree, where I'd feel safe from rabid cows. I'd done a lot of following, not the other way around, and watched Ike catch crawdads, eat worms, and dig tubers from the ground. He could climb trees, dig holes, and swim. I already knew he could play dead, and he was big and healthy. A strong little possum. He was as ready as I could make him.

Gran had made him a chocolate chip cookie for his going-away present. I knew the minute I set it down, he'd be all over it and I could sneak off. My eyes were watering, but that was because of the wind. I sniffed. *That* was dust. I wasn't going to cry.

I picked Ike up in my other hand and looked deep into his

eyes. He chittered at me as he caught the scent of the cookie. "I'll love you forever, bud. You be a good boy, now." I gently set him down right where we'd spent the last couple nights. I set the cookie down beside him, and after one last quick look I turned and ran for home. It was definitely the wind that brought tears to my eyes.

Gran met me at the door and gave me a big hug. I rubbed my tears against her shirt sleeve. "He's gone?" she said quietly.

"He's gone," I said, and turned to go take care of the chickens.

Everything I did the rest of the day felt like I was wading through body-high water. I couldn't concentrate, remembering where Blackie had done this or Ike had done that. The whole farm was taken over by memories, and I didn't like it one bit.

Mart had invited me over but I didn't want to go. I didn't want to stay inside because Mon and Gran were there and would keep looking at me, worrying about how I was holding up. I didn't want to write in my Lookbook. I wanted to stay away from everything. I didn't want to do anything anymore, and I couldn't stand it.

Gran was on the phone when I came back inside with my shirt full of eggs. As I finished filling some egg cartons, I heard her say, "Hold on." I froze, my hand dangling an egg midair. "It's your dad," she said, and held the phone out to me, her hand over the mouth piece. "You want to talk to him?" My mind skipped from Blackie to Loosy to Ike.

"No."

She shifted on her feet. "Are you sure?"

I shook my head.

"Why not? What should I tell him?"

I turned to her. "Tell him that when I *wanted* to talk to him on the phone, he didn't want to. And when Blackie died and I wrote him he didn't bother to write back. Even though Mon got a letter afterwards. *Now* he wants to talk to me?" I met her eyes, and as soon as I said it I knew it was really how I felt, and that made me feel good. "I have chores to finish." I left without waiting for her answer. I was proud of myself, though—I didn't even slam the door.

Once outside, I sat on the grass and stared out across the windswept prairie. A turkey buzzard was riding the wind high above me and I wished I could join him. This was the worst summer I'd ever had. I was so wrapped up in my thoughts that when little hands tugged on my shirt from behind I thought it was only another memory. I reached behind me and touched fur. And blinked. "Ike?" He chirred and chittered. I just stared at him.

Black eyes sparkled and he *cheh-cheh*'d at me. He seemed very happy with himself. How did he get back?

I knew I'd have to let him go again—but seeing him again made me overjoyed. I grabbed my backpack off the porch and lit off for the creek. I'd spend the day down there with him.

I blasted past the five cows, their babies startling in all directions like quail. Jezebel brayed at me, running alongside for a moment to kick up her heels before going back to her cow friends. I went even deeper into the pasture than I had before. There was a small round pond, with cattails and low trees drooping into the water. I didn't like this place so much on account of all the snakes, but Ike might like it because of them.

We spent the afternoon chasing minnows and catching baby turtles. Ike had fun eating them while I hung upside down from the trees around the pond. I didn't fall off but once or twice, and the pond was deep.

I finally set him down and he snuffled around my feet as I reached into my backpack. I'd leave him here tonight. I pulled out a few more chocolate chip cookies and laid them by his nose. He jumped on them with a chirr of delight and I was off, running. But this time I was sly. Once I got back to the little creek, I took a breath and stepped in, going to the middle and walking downriver. Maybe he'd get confused if he couldn't smell me on the ground. Rich black mud squished between my toes and covered my calf up to the knee as I walked. The creek couldn't wash that mud away, it was way too thick. When I was at the closest point to home I sloshed out, water sparkling in every direction, and ran to the house. After washing my legs at the tap, I went inside. Gran wasn't big on dirt.

I followed the sharp meaty smell of the barbecue to find Gran finishing setting the table. She smiled at me. "Where you been?" she asked casually, setting the baked potatoes on the table. I jumped up and took a seat.

"Creek."

Mon was already there and looked up at me as she speared a potato. "With Ike?"

She didn't need to be getting all up in my beeswax. It was none of her business. "Well, I might have seen him down there."

"Is it true, Fishstick? Your little friend staying down there?"

I hesitated but couldn't lie to my gran. "Mostly," I said, sliding my eyes away from her searching ones. "That's where I turned him loose."

She handed me the biscuit plate and I grabbed it but she didn't let it go. I tugged on it until I gave up and met her eyes.

"Honey, your mama and dad are coming home Wednesday."

"Wednesday?" Mon looked excited as Gran nodded.

"No problem," I said, biting into a biscuit. "Ike's gone for good."

Chapter 30

"Doggone it, you crazy possum!"

He was waiting by the garage door for me, chittering with good cheer as he danced around on his little pink feet. Even as I said it my spirits swooped up higher than the clouds. I couldn't stay mad at him.

I bent down and scooped him up, holding him close to my face. His nose pressed against mine and I just stood still a moment, feeling happy that he loved me enough to come find me.

At the same time I felt a hard sort of panic. This was the fourth time I'd released him into the wild, and he plainly didn't want to *be* wild—even though I mostly wanted him to be. I wanted him to be free and happy, but he loved me. Wasn't that enough of a reason to let a little possum come visiting? I sighed. It wouldn't be for my dad or my mama. Funny enough, it wasn't even a good enough reason for my gran.

She'd met me in my room the night before. After leaving him at the pond, he'd still found his way to me some hours later, chirring his happiness at finding me. He always found his way back.

"Princess."

"Yeah?"

"Honey, we have to talk about Ike." She sat on the edge of the bed, and I looked at her with heavy eyes. She sighed, looking down at her hands. "I don't know how to say this, heaven help me." She looked back up at me, her eyes searching. "You don't *really* want that possum to be free, do you?"

I didn't answer, and she went on. "If it were up to me, you could keep him. But it's so dangerous for him around here, what with your dad coming home, and Joe, and cars . . . ," she said, and I nodded.

"I know, Gran. I've tried and tried. But he loves me so much." She reached over, her wrinkled, lined old hand taking my tanned, scratched one.

"Fishstick, sometimes you have to let the things you love the most go so that they can live the life they're supposed to live. He's a wild animal, honey." Her other hand brushed my loose hair behind my ear. "If you want him safe, you're going to have to put the fear of the devil in him to make him stay away."

I didn't *want* him to stay away, that was the problem. I couldn't tell her that, the truth. Now, by the garage, I ruffled Ike's fur as I thought quickly. I was still wearing the bra, mostly because Mon said she never ever wanted it back and I'd found it was handy to carry all kinds of stuff in, like sandwiches. Ike chittered and rubbed his forehead against me, and his little fingers clenched my hand.

I'd have to go far, far away—down to the bottoms. I ran inside and grabbed some cookies and the phone, then held my breath as I dialed.

"Mart, it's me."

"What's going on?" He sounded like he was eating.

"Ike came back. Again."

The smacks quit and I was glad he was on the same page.

"Today's the day your dad and mama come home! What do you want me to do?"

"Listen, can you pick me up on your four-wheeler? I can't ride Jezebel. Joe is coming in two hours, and it'd take me that long just to catch her."

He swallowed. "Sure. As long as I don't have to get off anywhere."

"Nope. Just take me down to the bottoms. I haven't tried where . . . I found him. Maybe he'll be good there." Ike chittered and I shushed him as my gran walked past. "Can you come now?"

"I'm on my way."

When I opened the door, I nearly smacked into Gran. Her eyes dropped to my shirt and I knew she'd seen Ike. He hissed at her through the fabric. She paused while I watched my toe tracing the carpet. "You taking him somewhere else?"

"Mart's picking me up," I said, edging towards the door. "He's going to take me down to the bottoms. Maybe we'll have better luck there."

"They'll be here in a few hours, you know that? You've run out of time."

My stomach dropped. "I know, I know." Mart coasted into the driveway and I was off. This *had* to work.

Mart didn't slowpoke it around, either. You couldn't hear anything when the motor of the four-wheeler was running, so I just sat there watching the ground fly past as we headed for the deepest part of the bottoms. I clutched his arms as he navigated down the steep trail, zigzagging as he moved us down the hill. At the bottom, I sighed with relief.

"Back that way," I shouted, pointing in the direction of the peach tree. He nodded and gunned it, jouncing from grass hill to grass hill. When we got close enough, I tugged his arm to stop and he did. I slid off.

"I'll be back in a minute. Get ready to really hit it, okay?" He nodded again and left the engine running. I headed towards the darkest, shadiest part of the bottoms.

In a way, this was the best spot. This was where it had begun for all of us: Blackie, Ike, me. I was doing what I'd promised, and I hoped this time Ike would have the good sense to stay away from the house.

I layered the cookies in a cookie pyramid and hugged him to my neck, breathing in his musty smell. His hands scraped against my skin, clenching and unclenching as I pulled him away. He saw the pile of cookies below us and his eyes brightened.

I set him down. "Now stay here, do you hear?" I stamped my foot but it didn't keep him from grabbing a cookie. "You really can't come back. Dad'll get you. You be a good boy," I said, and lit out for Mart. He saw me coming and gunned the motor, and the moment I was on we headed off through the river bottoms, up the hill, and through the gate. In another fifteen minutes we were back home. I slid off.

"Thanks."

"No problem." He let his finger off the gas so it wasn't so loud and frowned at me. "Do you really think he's going to stay away?"

"I think so." Hopefully.

I waved at him as he left and entered a whirlwind of business inside the house. Mon came out of the bathroom and Gran, curlers jutting out every which way from her head, leaned out of Dad's room and yelled at me to get myself showered and ready.

Showtime.

Chapter 31

Joe showed up in his wife's four-door. It looked like it'd been cleaned up proper for once. It gleamed.

Joe, however, did not. He was still carrying his stupid gun.

"Joe," I said as I walked up to him, "what are you going to do with that gun at the airport? I'm pretty sure that that isn't allowed there, right?"

He pushed his hat back as Gran and Mon came outside, too, to greet him. "I reckon I'll just hide it in the car while I'm there." After a minute, he spoke up again. "Just wanted to be sure that nobody wanted to come along with me, to pick them up? Surprise them?"

Monica stepped forward faster than a shot and looked at Gran.

"I can go, right, Gran? Right? I've been good." She *had* been if you asked me. I could even stand her sometimes now. Gran nodded. Mon squealed and ran around to sit in the front seat.

I tugged at my shirt to straighten it.

Gran was giving Joe the flight information when Monica honked the horn. She honked it again, really leaning on it.

"What is going on, Monica? Do you want to stay here?" Gran hollered, angry, but Mon wasn't looking at her. She was waving her arms back and forth, her eyes fixed on me. When I looked at her, she pointed.

Across the lawn.

Oh please no, oh please no.

Ike was there, waddling towards us, his eyes trained on me. Right out across the lawn in front of Joe and everybody.

"Good Lord Almighty!" Joe said, and before I could say anything, he had the gun up and to his shoulder. In a blink.

"No!" Gran staggered towards him and the gun arm drooped as he stuck out a supporting hand to keep her from going over. I jumped in front of him with my arms out.

"*No*, Joe!" His expression hardened as he looked from me to the possum, and he tried to shove me out of the way with the front of the rifle. "It's got rabies, Princess! Get outta my way!"

I wasn't gonna stand for it anymore. I reached out, grabbed the front of the gun, and yanked it out of his hand with a force that caused him to stagger and lose his grip on Gran. The coolness of the iron burned me as I turned towards my possum. I raised up my arms, positioning it as I'd seen him do, time and time again. I started walking towards Ike.

Gran cried, "No!" but I shook my head, then forced the tip down and shot into the shale at my feet.

Something hit me, but I kept on walking. Something was burning. I heard screams behind me as the car door slammed, and I limped a little closer to my possum.

My heart just cracked. He was looking at me—with fear. Hatred. His eyes were wide, and his tongue came out of his mouth a little as he watched me. He'd seen me shoot the rifle. He'd hate me because I shot it. It was the only way to get him to stay away. Forever.

I stood still where he could focus on me and me alone. Blinking hard to get the tears out of my eyes, I tilted the gun down and shot it again. The echoing report shivered in my ears as I saw Ike open his mouth and hiss at me. His mouth was wide, and his teeth warned me away. Me, the evil one.

He turned around and hurried off, slithering into the bushes.

"The fear of the devil," I said, letting the rifle drop to my side. My leg was on fire, tiny rivers of pain sneaking up to meet the rivers exploding from my heart. I turned slowly to look at Joe. He was leaning over my gran, who lay on the gravel driveway. They all gawped at me in the sunlight, Mon's eyes traveling down to my leg. Then she started puking.

My vision kept blinking in and out. Dark. Light. Dark. I could hardly see through my tears. I choked a little. *He was my pet. He loved me.*

I lifted the gun and tossed it aside as hard as I could. It bounced and skittered along the ground. "I *never* want to see this gun on my property *ever, ever again!*" I screamed.

Chapter 32

I stared at the other end of the room. I'd been doing it ever since I woke up here, all alone, and remembered what happened. Or parts of it.

It was an ugly room. A vomit yellow color on the walls with real tacky pictures of flowers, of all things. A big wide window with one of those school-type air conditioners that were always set too cold.

At least I wasn't too close to the window. I didn't want to see outside. I didn't want to have anything to do with anything, really.

People kept coming in to talk to me—even Mr. Sugna's wife, who ended up being a nurse here—but I didn't say anything. Just would sigh and turn my face to the wall, ignoring their caring soft words, their voices. Until they left.

My eyes started to leak again, and I used the top of my hospital gown to wipe them away.

Turns out Gran had fallen when Joe'd let go of her and she'd broken her hip, and they'd had to cram us both into the city ambulance to get into town. Mon had to stay behind. There hadn't been enough space in the ambulance for her.

My leg twitched under the cover. They'd managed to pick all the buckshot out although I'd likely have scars there. A human Appaloosa, skin scars instead of hair spots. That didn't count the heart scars either. They'd given me enough medicine to knock a horse down, so I couldn't tell you how long I'd been here. But nothing they gave me canceled out the pain.

"P?"

I knew that voice. I sat up and stared at the doorway.

Mr. Sugna stood centered in it, shifting from foot to foot. He was about the last person I would expect to come visit me but my heart eased up a little. He'd known Ike too.

"Should—I go, *chérie*?"

"Naw, come in." My voice sounded quiet and dried up.

He stepped inside slowly, his long whiskery eyebrows wiggling like a butterfly's antennae. He had something clenched in his hand. "How are you, *chérie*? How is your leg?"

"Ike's gone, Mr. Sugna." I could feel the burning that warned me of tears, but they didn't come. I didn't think I had any more water left to cry with. "I didn't want him to go, not really. I know I said I did, but I lied. He was my pet and I loved him."

Mr. Sugna stretched out the other arm and snagged a chair, bringing it over to sit by me. He sighed. "But you let him be free, *chérie*. Free as he should be. Even though it hurt,"—he paused—"him . . . and you."

"My dad won't be happy with me at all," I said. That was an understatement. He'd likely ground me for the rest of my life. First having a possum, then shooting Joe's gun, and he'd probably pin Gran's broken hip on me too.

Mr. Sugna smiled and shook his head. "But what you must think of first," he said, "is are *you* happy with you? You did what you said you would do even if it hurt, you did what you thought was right. That is most important, *non*?"

I hadn't thought about it like that. I lay there staring at my hands until he got up and bent over. "Here." He reached down and opened my hand, putting something hard and angled into it before shutting it back tight. "This is for you. I am proud of you, P. I believe you did the right thing." He smiled again and left.

I cracked open my fingers. A little clay possum stared up at me, perfect in its likeness to Ike. I learned I wasn't all cried out after all. Mr. Sugna was right: I had done what I thought best. My dad didn't have to like what I'd done, but Ike was free and safe because of me.

Mr. Sugna popped his head back in, and I jumped. "Preen-cess, your papa, he is at the end of the hall. He is worried you do not want to see him." Mr. Sugna stepped inside the room and twisted his hands into knots as his eyebrows wiggled. "Should I bring him here, *chérie*?"

I wiped my tears. "No, Mr. Sugna." I took a deep breath. "I'll go for him." I'd done the right thing by Ike. Now I could do the same by my dad.